Everything
Affects
Everyone

Shawna Lemay

Palimpsest Press
1171 Eastlawn Ave.
Windsor, Ontario, N8S 3J1
www.palimpsestpress.ca

Printed and bound in Canada
Cover design and book typography by Ellie Hastings
Edited by Aimée Dunn
Copyedited by Theo Hummer

Palimpsest Press would like to thank the Canada Council for the Arts and the Ontario Arts Council for their support of our publishing program. We also acknowledge the assistance of the Government of Ontario through the Ontario Book Publishing Tax Credit.

LIBRARY AND ARCHIVES CANADA CATALOGUING IN PUBLICATION

TITLE: Everything affects everyone / Shawna Lemay.
NAMES: Lemay, Shawna, 1966- author.
IDENTIFIERS: Canadiana (print) 20210271027
            Canadiana (print) 20210271035
            Canadiana (ebook) 20210271035

ISBN 9781989287842 (SOFTCOVER)
ISBN 9781989287927 (EPUB)
ISBN 9781989287941 (PDF)

CLASSIFICATION: LCC PS8573.E5358 E94 2021 | DDC C813/.54—DC23

For Rob and Chloe

Be patient toward all that is unsolved in your heart and try to love the questions themselves, like locked rooms and like books that are now written in a very foreign tongue. Do not now seek the answers, which cannot be given you because you would not be able to live them. And the point is, to live everything. Live the questions now. Perhaps you will then gradually, without noticing it, live along some distant day into the answer.

—Rainer Maria Rilke

We need to be angels for each other, to give each other strength and consolation. Because only when we fully realize that the cup of life is not only a cup of sorrow but also a cup of joy will we be able to drink it.

—Henri J.M. Nouwen

A long silence trails behind them that's how you can recognize there are angels.

—Anna Kamienska

The life of every person is susceptible to a painful deepening and the life of every person is "unbelievable."

—Clarice Lispector

I can only count on my own wings. I unsheathed them. Crumpled, two leaves of paper. Will I suffice?

—Hélène Cixous

All human beings experience annunciation. With pregnant souls we raise our hands to our throats with surprise and anguish. As if each of us had learned at a given moment in life that we have a mission to fulfill. That mission is by no means easy: each of us is responsible for the entire world.

—Clarice Lispector

.

Daphne and Xaviere

The day of Daphne's funeral, I'd taken great care to dress in something she might like, just as I would have if we were going out for coffee. I wore a bracelet she'd always admired and a scarf I could imagine her reaching over and touching— she'd have admired the texture and colours and would have leaned over and delicately fingered the knotted fringe.

Daphne and I had been friends, though not close friends, for several years. We'd met in a first-year university art history class and had kept in touch afterwards. I had profoundly believed that Daphne and I would end up as close friends and that we'd mean something to each other over the long term. I hadn't known there was so little time, or I would have looked at her more closely and seen, to echo the short story by Marquez, the ungainly flapping: her wings, slipping on the light, trying to gain purchase on the air.

We were to hold each other to our dreams. I was to be a poet and a librarian; I wanted to be alone and lonely and experience all those dark and dazzling reveries a young poet should accumulate. I wanted to sit with my own questions, to come to love them, and to live with them. And she was going to be a talk show host and write a children's book, and we'd agreed to remind each other of that until we had become these magical-sounding beings.

Our boyfriends at the time knew each other and were friends. We had several friends in common. We'd see each other at parties, and once in a while we went out for coffee with each other. Long intervals would pass and we wouldn't see each other at all. I relied on bumping into her in our favourite clothing store on Whyte Avenue, or in Café le Gare, now a bar, across from the train station.

A couple years after graduation, I was between jobs and probably about to lose my crumby apartment and was sort of mentally drifting. I'd broken up with my fellow, and so had little contact with Daphne or her boyfriend. When I got the call from her boyfriend, Joel, it was the first time I'd talked to him on the phone. He told me she'd died and there would be a funeral, and also that he had something from her for me. I couldn't speak after he told me this, and he couldn't speak either, so we breathed into our phones and said nothing for ages. Eventually he whispered, "Xaviere?" and I said, "Yes."

And, "How?"

"Remember how she fainted all the time over anything, and everyone thought it was cute or funny or like some kind of cool party trick?"

"Uh-huh," I said.

"Well, it was a sign that she had a heart condition, and she died of a heart attack."

She was too young—too young for a heart attack, too young to die—and I was selfish. I wanted more of her and now I didn't have her. And neither did Joel.

I went to her funeral, which was beautiful in the way that funerals for young people are beautiful. The unfairness. The shattering of everything. The music is more meaningful, the poems, the readings. Everyone is crying as quietly and as quickly as possible so as to make it less intolerable for the others. Nothing seems real and you get to experience that— how nothing seems possible or true and everything is black, but your own young life is suddenly a light. Blazing.

What a big, weird, awful shame it was, I kept thinking to myself during the funeral. A shame that she couldn't listen to all the beautiful music and poetry and know how loved she was. And selfishly, I wanted her back, because I felt as though I'd barely gotten to know her. She seemed to know so many talented people; they were obviously drawn to her. The cellist who played Elgar was a childhood friend who'd flown in from Detroit, where she'd been playing with the DSO. The poet, who was said to be a protégée of the American Poet Laureate Howard Nemerov, recited Auden's "Funeral Blues"— "Stop all the clocks, cut off the telephone…"—and began by recounting how she and Daphne had played together at a hotel pool in Spain when they were eleven. Their parents had each taken them on vacation, and it turned out they were all from Edmonton, and back home they all became fast friends. The families had dinner together on the first Tuesday of every month; still did, still would, in her memory.

Daphne also had a friend in med school, friends who were visual artists, friends who were travelling the world and working for NGOs, friends who were aspiring politicians. I couldn't help wondering what she had seen in me at all.

Afterwards, we ate crustless sandwiches with her relatives, listened to people talk through their tears, and watched everyone shake their heads and say all the usual things, but with great feeling and heavy disbelief. A lot of people hung out around the edges of the room and were silent, sipping the awful coffee, and on my way out I noticed a barge filled with lipstick-stained white cups, half empty, which seemed to me to be an image Daphne would have adored.

Daphne was an only child and her parents, Fred and Lucy, were not taking it well. Why should they?

As I was leaving, Joel handed me a package wrapped in brown paper: cassettes. Three stacks, wrapped in plastic wrap, then brown paper, and with red and white string around it like a package from the deli. There were thirty of them, I

would later discover. "It's a series of interviews with an elderly photographer she'd been working with who'd passed on near the end, maybe before she'd finished, not sure," he said. He was hoping I would transcribe them so that all her work wouldn't be lost. By then, most of us had switched to CDs, and cassettes were older technology, already being abandoned.

I was not surprised to hear she was working on something; she'd always had a pet project on the go and had since she was a kid. When she was in elementary school, she had made an elaborate chart of all the places the Grade Fours had lived and travelled and where they wanted to one day travel. What was interesting, she said, was the power of suggestion: if one child said they had been born in Egypt, another would list Egypt as somewhere they wished to travel.

As a teenager, for quite a while, she was interested in birthday parties and would take notes on people's childhood memories of parties, whether they were joyous or traumatic or unusual. She would take down details about the parties themselves—where they were held, the descriptions of cakes and flavours of frosting, presents received and the colours and patterns of the paper in which they were wrapped, the photographs taken of the children, the games played, the locations, and even things like the patterns of tablecloths. Anything a person could remember. She'd also note the expressions on the person's face as they recounted the memories and how they seemed afterwards—happy, introspective, subdued. She would ask them things afterwards like, "Do you enjoy birthday parties now?" "How was it to select and give the gift?" If they had children, she'd ask, "Do you have similar parties for your own children?" And she'd ask, "What sort of memory is this for you?"

She had interviewed a friend of the family, a man in his thirties. She noted what he was wearing the day she spoke with him, his surprise at the random flow of memories, especially at certain ones. "I'd not thought of that in years and

years," he'd said, speaking of a gift he'd received of plastic animal figurines all bundled in a netting. "And the cake was angel food with whipped cream for frosting with sprinkles poured liberally over top of it." He'd wanted a huge bundle of colourful balloons but didn't get them. The memory of the disappointment, and trying to hide the disappointment, was acute. But even more strongly recalled was that instead of a bouquet of balloons, a friend of his had brought him an orange one filled with helium. What joy that balloon had brought him!

Another woman remembered kissing a boy at her best friend's party. "It was Junie Watson's party, and I was jealous because of the all the things she was getting. The latest doll, the most adorable frock, and a new board game. So I went into the backyard, and one of the boys (who lived two doors down and whom her mother had made her invite) was standing there and we sat on the back stoop and he kissed me. Twice." She'd touched her lips throughout the whole interview, smoothing them, then patting, then tapping, then smoothing again. Daphne said she wrote notes about what the woman wore the day she talked to her: a pink wool car coat and a floral scarf in pastels. When she'd kissed the boy, she'd been wearing a baseball t-shirt with red sleeves and rainbow jeans. She'd worn the same thing nearly every day that summer, she said.

Daphne liked to be thorough, but when I asked her why she did this, she just laughed and said, "I don't really know. It's fun. A bit sad, too. Good practice." And then, after an interval, she said, "I want to take care of them. I want them to know that I'm responsible for them. It's an Annunciation."

I didn't know what she meant by *annunciation*. The truth is she was genuinely interested in people, interested in knowing how things were with them, and she came to understandings by focusing in on one particular thing. "You can find out anything that way," she said. "Ask a person about something they're not expecting to talk about, or about a memory—it's

a way of getting at how they feel about the world. The topic itself is almost incidental. Almost." She had a way of knowing what the "not quite incidental" topic might be, a sixth sense for finding the topic that would spark memories.

This was how we'd met, in our first-year art history course. She had wanted to work on a project in more depth. At that point, I'd lived in Edmonton my entire life and had only left it to go on family vacations to Disneyland. My experience with viewing art was minimal. I'd been to the Edmonton Art Gallery a couple of times; the cold, concrete two-story building it was then, before it was razed and rebuilt as a modern structure in the 2000s, was known as a textbook example of Brutalist architecture. I remember sitting in the main-floor gallery looking at huge abstract paintings and feeling so cool and critical, as if my opinions mattered. I had so little to base them on at that point.

Daphne had wanted people to talk about how they felt when looking at paintings. She conducted her research in two parts. She interviewed some people while they were at the art gallery, as they were looking. There was silence on the tape, there was a shuffling of feet, the sound of high heels walking by and into the distance on the hard floor, unknown whooshing and swishing, and, at times, crinkly feedback from going too close to the microphone. She'd ask quiet questions, as though they were in a church. And the person would answer back quietly, too.

The second part of her research was asking a person to recall seeing a favourite painting from anywhere in the world. Some really enjoyed spinning out the story and talking about where and when they'd travelled to Paris or London or Athens. They talked about the museum and what they liked about it and how difficult or how easy it was to get to. Others just talked very directly about their encounter with a particular painting. How they had seen themselves in a particular image, or felt some kind of spiritual connection, or that their breathing had increased and they had felt faint or dizzy. One had seen

a still life that captivated, and she had kept going back to it and even made a special trip back the next day to the museum to see it. Though she had never drawn anything (not since grade school) and didn't consider herself to have any talent in that area, she had sat down and sketched the painting all one morning, page after page, compelled to by forces unknown, by this feeling that she had to get *into* the work somehow, to crawl in by means of this sketching, scratching.

Daphne had asked me one day after class if I'd like to be part of this series of interviews she was doing about art. At the time it seemed edgy, and I wanted to be thought of as edgy and cool and interesting. I had said yes, slowly, reservedly, even though the word had jumped into my head even as she was speaking. Yes.

"I like to do these interviews," she said, "in public places, because the ambient noise adds to the tone of the piece." We went to the Café la Gare and sat by the big, murky, condensation and frost-filled windows near the street, and she'd hauled the bright orange tape recorder out of her bag and popped it on the table, sideways at first, so it took up less space. We took turns getting our own coffees.

When we'd both had a sip or two, she set it in the center of the table and gave it a pat, then pressed the button. "Let's begin with the name of the painting, the artist."

When we started, she'd glanced at her watch and noted the time. As she interviewed me, she took notes. I had bought a carrot muffin and at one point took a nibble. She scribbled a quick word or two without looking down at the page. Across the table her writing seemed illegible, cryptic. Her script was small and unusual. Later, I would become a bit of an expert in deciphering it, but then I couldn't have read it, unless maybe I had turned her notebook around or held it up and squinted.

After we'd finished, she clicked the stop button on the compact recorder. She sat and, without saying anything, jotted notes. She had seemed so absorbed that, as awkward as

I felt, I didn't feel I could interrupt or stare too hard at what she was writing.

When at last she had finished up, she told me that she was just trying to capture the ambient noises, in case they weren't clear on tape. She'd also tried to capture what the silences might have been. A hesitation, perhaps, a stoppage. When the woman behind us had taken a long time getting out of her down-filled coat and untwining the long wool scarf from her neck and all of the unusual raspy noises ensued, Daphne's expression had become buoyant, even as the interview went on uninterrupted. The chair was scraped out, the texture of the coat had its own sound, the sound of her book thunking down on the table, the woman's loud sigh uttered to the universe.

At one point, as we were talking, there was an accident in the kitchen and a cup or plate shattered, followed by some cursing and then some laughter. The café suddenly became quiet, and then quickly, the noise returned to fill the brief lull.

Daphne told me that she liked keeping all this extraneous clatter rather than cleaning up the interview. And when she would transcribe it, she liked to note the messy, unplanned, unconnected bits. "It's part of the music," she'd said, "part of the score." And, "Often my favourite part of the tape is the beginning, right after the big square button is pushed and engaged. There's that odd crackling and the tape itself starts to breathe. No one speaks for a bit. You can hear paper being organized, or one last sip of water or coffee being taken. A few deep breaths. There's the sound of pages or wings ruffling, like the two humans are fluttering a little, flying about, helplessly attempting to attain flight (is it an attempt at escape, she whispered, or the beginning of an annunciation?), then folding their wings up, tucking them in."

After the funeral, I returned home to my apartment, placed the package of tapes on the kitchen table. When CDs had made their appearance, I'd switched over as soon as I could afford a player, and my cassette deck was buried in

a box in my storage closet. The tapes just sat there in the center of the table collecting dust for a while. I studiously ignored them when I ate my breakfast cereal in the morning and as I sat in front of them with my dinner, a fried egg and toast that I dipped into the yolk. One day, months after Daphne's funeral, they confronted me. I had been on the couch reading poetry—Anne Sexton—lying on my back, one leg crooked over the other. My neck was a little sore from resting on the arm, my attention absorbed in my book. I'd been repeating the line: "Put your ear down close to your soul and listen hard."

The sun had aligned itself with my kitchen window, and also with my kitchen table. And when I happened to rouse myself from my reading reverie and looked over from my low vantage point, the tower of cassette boxes was illuminated; the dust motes hung and hovered and trembled above them like magisterial creatures.

I went to the closet and dug around for the box with my cassette player. I unravelled the cord from a string of Christmas lights and from around the legs of a ceramic elephant statue.

As soon as I pushed the button and it engaged, I heard the silence that was not at all silent—I knew there was something unanswerable about what I was about to hear. First there was the sound of birds trapped in a hayloft; then a door swung open and they left, their wings flapping close together. When the dialogue began, it took a while for a voice, then voices, to separate from the rest of the sound, to be distinguishable.

Daphne: I'm in a house on the road which leads to Lake Isle in Alberta. I'm speaking today, April 4th, 1991, with the photographer Irene Guernsey.

After this, there was a deliberate pause, as though the two women were deciding whether or not to proceed, to break the silence, to delve and to reveal.

I listened to the first couple of minutes of the conversation, stopped the tape, and immediately phoned Joel and asked him if there were notebooks, too. There were too many things I was hearing that I couldn't identify. Also, I had underestimated how moving, how devastating it would be to hear Daphne's voice again.

Daphne: You've never given an interview before.
Irene: I've refused.
D: You never wanted to clarify the work?
I: The work resists clarification.
D: Okay.
I: Talking about your own work is dangerous to the artistic process.
D: In what ways?
I: I'm not trying to be enigmatic but have wished to guard the mystery of the work, of my particular work, and those things I have been in the presence of, and which I am obligated to preserve.

I went to Daphne's parents' house and they took me to the garage, where there were plastic boxes filled with her past projects. They were all perfectly labelled, so it was easy to find everything that pertained to Irene. There were boxes marked, "looking at art," and there were boxes simply labelled, "Irene Guernsey." Fred and Lucy were happy enough to see them go. You could see they were overwhelmed, months after the funeral. Like it was all really just starting to sink in. And they seemed to be walking around in two separate dimensions. In one, they looked as though they could break down and fold up, falling into a deep fairy-tale sleep. But in the other, they were gracious hosts, interested in what I had to say and asking me, with real support, what I intended to do with the material.

"I'm sorry to say we're not exactly sure what's even in the boxes," said Lucy. "Of course, you're welcome to them. Daphne always had some line of inquiry on the go,

sometimes more than one. Even when she was little, she had projects and lists and she spent time interviewing her stuffed animals, you know. We always imagined she'd go on and be a news anchor, or a Barbara Walters type."

I thought Lucy was going to break down at this point, but she'd had practice bringing herself back from that other dimension, and instead she shook her shoulders and leaned in to give my arm a squeeze. "There's soup," she said and turned, not giving me a chance to say no. I sat at the cozy table in Daphne's parents' kitchen and had soup and bread and banana cake, which had been timed to come out of the oven when we'd finished our lunch. So we had coffee before we started talking about her again. At some point, Daphne's father left, and there was just me and Lucy sitting at the kitchen table.

"Women talking," she said. "There has not been enough work done on how women talk, the meanings that can be found in the tracery around the words themselves. Do you know what I mean?"

I nodded yes, without really understanding.

"The way we come to a conversation matters. The openness, the trust. I know these are things that Daphne was interested in. Is every conversation a type of annunciation? Each person is an angel giving the other person, who is also an angel, a message. In that moment we are each responsible for the other. If one of the people in the conversation were to faint or to cry, for example, it would be up to the other person to act."

"Okay," I said. "Yes."

"If a person were injured, even soul-injured…"

"Yes."

"If you find a bird with an injured wing…"

"I see what you mean."

Daphne and Irene and Xaviere

I began transcribing.

Daphne: In one of your photos there's a child, it seems to be a boy, wearing shorts and no shirt, running through the forest, a glimpse of the lake beyond. The figure is blurred and there are trees everywhere, but you've caught the runner at a perfect point of visibility in this thicket. And there is something very mysterious about this black-and-white photo. Viewing it, I wanted to get very close and examine the bark of the trees and the leaves. For a while one forgets about the child before being irresistibly drawn back. There's a stillness around the boy; the air around him takes on a shape. His arms, pumping, a blur. He seems to be running out of his shoulder blades. Am I seeing this correctly?

Irene: Photographing is a way of coming to understand how seeing works. We see through a lens differently. This is because the lens might allow in vibrations and feelings, silence and space and time, things we experience but which can be fleeting, which can pass us by and even pass through us, before we have time to examine them.

D: Do you remember taking this photograph?

I: I waited. This is also a photograph about waiting; all my photographs have this element. I went into the woods with just the camera. Of course, all photographers are always waiting, even when they don't have a camera strung around their neck.

D: Do you use a tripod?

I: No. I've always needed the weight of the camera in my hands, around my neck. It's very centering.

I went into the woods, entering it from a position a distance from the lake. I walked toward the lake then, waiting for it to be viewable through the trees, but only barely. There's a fallen tree, and I'm sitting on it, and I'm looking. There's a path through the trees farther on where the boy later runs. And I find that there's one clear shot through the trees. There are lake cottages, you see, away from the lake in rows, small ones, full of families. And most people walk down the road to get to the lake, but there's also this path. It's worn, but the branches hang over in places. There are more mosquitoes if you walk through the trees.

D: So this was very planned—orchestrated, in a way.

I: No, nothing was ever orchestrated. Hoped for, yes, but never orchestrated.

D: Right, right.

[Here there is silence for a moment or two. There's the sound of a cup being lifted from a table and later being put back down. There's a soft thump, and each of the women laughs a little. A cat has entered the room and settled on Irene's lap and begun to purr. The purring can be heard throughout the next part of the tape and then tapers off and disappears. Perhaps the cat has quietly left.]

D: Shall we continue? Okay. When I look at your photographs, I find I blink frequently. As though I just missed something that flew through the frame. And maybe blinking is a kind of reaction to feeling one has missed something

special or wonderful or even kind of rare. So there's this feeling of regret, but also hope—that whatever it was will appear in a subsequent image. I want to keep looking even as I feel loss. I'm sorry, I'm talking too much. And we've just begun.

I: I kept thinking I'd seen something that I couldn't have seen and didn't want to say. I needed proof. I felt I needed proof, though I didn't need it for myself.

D: Is this when you started taking photos?

I: Oh no. I'd been at it for years. Practicing.

D: And suddenly you weren't practicing?

I: Exactly. I think it was with this particular image of the boy running through the forest that I became an artist.

I stopped the tape here because it reminded me of a conversation I'd had with Daphne. I had asked her what she thought was a good question and what she liked about asking questions and also about the way in which photographs were like questions. We talked about those things that must be in place before an interview is conducted, if one hopes for moments of truth and small revelations to occur, before the most important or interesting question may be asked. We talked about Jane Austen's famous line, and those things Edmond Jabès said in a conversation with Paul Auster. We were sitting on a couch in the front window of the trendy imported-clothing store on Whyte Avenue near the university. The couch had thin rugs and thick blankets thrown all over it. She'd taken two books out of her backpack and kept knocking them together, the Austen and the Auster. She first opened up the Austen:

In *Emma*, "Seldom, very seldom, does complete truth belong to any human disclosure; seldom can it happen that something is not a little disguised, or a little mistaken…"

And then Jabès, with his observations on how when two people are talking, "one of them must remain silent… Now, during this silence that you impose on yourself, you are all the while forming questions and answers in your mind, since

you can't keep interrupting me. And as I continue to speak, you are eliminating questions from your mind…"

We talked about how Jabès admits that he is "more concerned with interiority than description. It is the questioning around the story that gives the story its dimension. But the story is there only as a kind of basic pretext."

And it was here that Daphne said, "I think this is why I can't stop asking questions. Because you never know where the questions will lead, and so the narrative in a long conversation that takes place in many sittings isn't like the plot of a book, because it constantly leads the questioner into the unknown. As soon as you begin to wish for a particular outcome, you eliminate the possibilities of revelations unfathomed.

"And if it *is* like the writing of a novel, this pushing forward into the unknown, it's with the knowledge that one can't go back and re-arrange or polish or edit.

"The story, if there even is one, reveals itself without authorial intervention, without the falseness of the shaping, ordering, and arranging of events so that they conform to a schedule of narrative expectations, such as one is taught in school.

"The balance in many novels is weighted heavily on the side of plot… but when I read, I'm always looking for those works that give the interior priority. I want to know what characters are thinking and how they attempt to speak what's in their soul, honestly and simply. Or, alternatively, how they circle around things, how they attempt to conceal, or how they fail to express what they mean to convey."

We went back and forth; perhaps I murmured and encouraged. Some of the following observations might even be mine, but they came out of things she said. I would never have even thought about them had she not instigated this conversation about conversations. Things we said, though credit belongs mostly Daphne I believe, went something like this:

"Okay, it can get messy, and an interview can go off the rails if it's not carefully planned, but then if it's planned too

carefully, the risk is that it's dull and safe and simply feeds into the interviewer's expectations. So although such a conversation might seem formless, there is a basic shape that one arrives at in the end."

"Sometimes when a conversation moves forward into another space, it can be harrowing or traumatic. Sometimes a conversation will move into a future that neither person will yet understand. They will move into a space that only years later they will have a full understanding of. The ideas will be too new or too radical. Even the speakers don't know what to do with them quite yet."

"Some conversations are unequal, weighted heavily to one speaker, and this is okay depending on circumstances, understandings, histories. On one occasion, this person talks the most, and on the next, the other will be dominant."

"I'm interested in those things that silence us in everyday conversation. For example, the other person goes on too long until we feel we cannot speak. We've become listeners instead, audience members. We might feel less important. The one who listens becomes increasingly reticent, acquiesces. When at last we're called on to speak, to rejoin the conversation, it may be too late. The scene has shifted. Our courage to speak has been tamped down. Or, we're bored. The conversation has collapsed."

"The breathing of listening is different from the breathing we do when talking. A conversation takes on a rhythm and has its own breathing. Each person relies on the inhalations and exhalations of the other."

"An interview differs from a conversation because the interviewer has researched and knows certain things about the subject. The interviewee usually knows little and often

nothing about the interviewer but quickly learns about their stance from body language, the tone and quality of the questions. Sometimes the interviewer would like to set their subject at ease, and at other times keep them guessing, keep them nervous and alert."

"If the interviewer hasn't a well-known reputation, then perhaps she begins by gaining the trust of her subject—if this is the goal, and it is for me—by paying attention to one's own facial expressions, to how one dresses, even to the quality of equipment and one's handling of it. It might be necessary to set the subject at ease by showing that one has done one's research, immediately revealing something you know about them."

"An interview can transform and become a conversation. There's nothing stopping it."

I wonder what she'd say about my role. The role of the third party, the eavesdropper, the listener, the unknown and perhaps even unimagined audience. I suppose she'd note that in the situation of a taped interview, that person is present even in their absence. When two people talking in a room turn on a recording device, immediately their tone will change, even if slightly. There is an awareness of the third unknown presence, which each might imagine differently. One might imagine another particular person listening in, or a small group. And the other might imagine their words and voices being broadcast on the radio.

When I first began listening to the tapes, knowing that both of the speakers were no longer with us, I felt I was in the presence of ghosts. When I began transcribing, I felt responsible in a way I wouldn't have had they been alive.

I felt I could see the photographs being described. The interviews kept coming back to particular images, and I felt the need to see them, to spend time with them.

D: You have exhibited your photographs, but not often.

I: I was never particularly appreciated. Never in demand.

[Laughs.]

D: And yet you were compelled to show the work.

I: I suppose I wished to see how other people felt when they viewed my work. Did they see what I did? Not that I would ever ask them, not that I would want to enter into that private exchange between viewer and photograph. The artist has no business in that space. That's an entirely different kind of conversation.

D: Did you ever write an artist statement to accompany any of the shows you had? I'm thinking of the exhibit at Henderson Gallery.

I: I don't want to tell people what to see. Not in my photographs. Not anywhere. What I would say now, is that, looking back, I wanted people to be open to not knowing, to doubt.

D: And what is your own experience of doubt?

I: Ah, doubt, the doubt of the artist is apart from the doubt in the viewer. Because. Because, the doubt of seeing is different from the doubt of creating...

Let me say that there were intervals when I didn't have time for doubt; my project consumed me. And working in secrecy helps. I didn't have cause to show my work or even talk about it for years at a time. There was a tremendous freedom in this. It's quite possible that we talk too much about our work these days. There is too much talk and not enough making. There is not enough thinking about art. The viewers wish the artist to do that work for them. But there is also the feeling that the work will disappear if the artist doesn't immediately erect a cloud of words around the art.

D: Who were the artists and photographers that were in your circle of friends?

I: Though I was open to meeting other photographers, it never happened, wasn't possible. Outside of the nearest large city, it's too isolated. And even when I went to galleries and art shows in the city, meetings were only superficial. Artists and photographers don't necessarily mix well, perhaps. Or maybe it was just me.

D: Shall I pour you some more tea?

I: Just a little, then.

[There is the sound of tea being poured, a clatter when the pot is set back down and upsets a spoon balanced on a saucer. Someone murmurs about the small table. A sip is taken, cups set back down.]

D: Have you felt quite alone then, in your art?

I: I'd always had an unrequited desire to have conversations with another living person about art. Even as I have felt myself unequal to such discussions, and am likely increasingly unable to talk about art because I've internalized things for so long. But yes, the fantasy of sitting in a room of intellectuals and artists or poets and being part of that has persisted, even in a subdued way. The fantasy has persisted. I'm not sure there's any real scene in the cities near here, or Bloomsbury-type groups, and if there is, I'm not a part of it or them. But the serious artists are working. I was once invited to join a group of artists and photographers who met at a lounge once a week as a standing order. They were all amateurs, poseurs. Which sounds terrifically snobby, but I think we both know what I mean by this. Anyone who has been around the art world knows. And honestly, I've nothing against those who dabble, nothing against amateurs. I encourage them, I do. I commend them. But they can clutter up the atmosphere. Confuse. Do you know? Their art confuses people who know too little already about what's good, what's worthy of spending time with, what's real. Of course, we all start out that way. So.

Or, here is another answer to your question. Wait.

Another answer is that I am utterly alone in my work. The artist is utterly alone, is a secret truth. If you are not alone, perhaps you are not an artist.

D: Do you believe that?

I: I don't know.

Listening, it's not always possible to tell when a session ends or begins. But in this case, the tape recorder has been turned on and then forgotten. There is the rustling of paper and then faraway talk. *Can I get you some water, my dear? Are you comfortable? We'll have a dish of ice cream afterwards.* There is the sound of general movement, settling in. A notebook opening. A deep breath. A soft clearing of the throat. Daphne says, *Shall we?* And this is perhaps where she notices she has already absently pushed the record button. There is an electronic kerfuffle for a second as she adjusts the machine. And then they begin.

D: Let me describe a few of your photographs and then we can talk about them. Would this be alright?

I: Of course.

D: There is a girl balancing on a fallen tree, coming toward the viewer. Her arms are raised, less for balance, more in an act of play or pretend. A girl with very long blonde hair is twirling and you've caught her mid-twirl, her hair a swirling mass behind her, and it's as though the hair is an entity unto itself, flying. A boy with long hair running fast through the trees, his hair a blur behind him. In another image, there is a girl and a boy, and they are standing facing each other, their arms outstretched, hands palm to palm. Were these posed or arranged photographs?

I: Heavens no, not at all.

D: But they look as though they could be. Do you worry that people will think otherwise?

I: First I will say this. That it's difficult to talk about one's own art. Yet we're asked to, and there are times when it's

truest to say *I don't know* or *it's not my business* or *it would be better to leave that as mysterious.* Instead, the artist has to look at their art as a critic might, or a scholar, and offer some insight after the fact, which I think can ruin the artist's feelings about the making of a piece and even skew what goes on creatively from that point. It's a profound thing to be constantly immersed in a process and never have to come out of it to look at things from a different angle. This heightens the creative process, you see.

D: Oh, yes.

I: The children knew me. Their parents knew me. Not well, but they knew I took photographs. I was never without my camera. I suppose I became invisible over time, each summer. Of course there was this sort of condescension where I was concerned. In that community. I was the woman who lived alone at the defunct pheasant farm. There were still a few pheasants—I kept the few goldens because they were odd and beautiful, and the game birds, the ring-necked ones, there were some that just lived, outside the pens, and I fed them. But I no longer *kept* them.

D: How did you end up here, on a pheasant farm?

I: A long, dull story. It belonged to my lover whose wife lived in the city and wanted no part of rural life. But someone had to look after the birds, the land, the house, and so I was officially the gamekeeper. We had agreed our relationship would only take place a couple of days per week, usually on week days. This left me the time and space to photograph all the weekend people, as I thought of them. Those who lived away and had so-called real houses in the city.

D: You were a kept woman?

[Laughter from both.]

I: Yes. No, honestly. I was in a position where I needed little, where I could make my art and think about art. Which is something any artist needs—time to think about what she is

making, about the world into which her art is arriving, about existence, how and why we are here. Eventually, the relationship ended and he sold me this place for next to nothing.

D: In history, the facts of a woman artist's life must include how she sustained herself. Would you agree?

I: Upon her death, I'd been left the family farm by my mother. My father had passed away much earlier. In that regard, I was fortunate enough to be an only child. I sold the farm—very good land, sought after—and invested the money. I can tell you they wouldn't have approved of the selling, or my life, my taking photographs. They wouldn't have understood. We have very few family photos. There are very few of me as a child, even.

D: Some photographers work in series. Or it ends up that way. You can look back at a body of work and groupings emerge. There are periods in the work. I'm thinking of photographers like Sally Mann, for example.

I: I was always working with a single obsession which consumed me. And I didn't have a spotlight on what I was doing like Sally Mann did. Nor was I photographing my own children. Eventually hers grew up, and so her family series would naturally come to a close. But I was constantly looking at the lake and its environs, including those who came to the lake every summer, and sometimes in the winter.

D: You knew of her work? Did it influence your own?

I: Of course. Even if I hadn't known about her work it would still have influenced my own. Influence can be like that—invisible, unknown. It's in the air and has powers unconnected to those who are in its sway.

In any case, at times my photographs weren't about the photograph at all. The camera gave me an excuse to pursue, to think without thinking, to think via images. The camera can be a red herring, you know. I wanted to see, to know by seeing.

D: But what exactly was it you wanted to see? There was something, wasn't there?

I: Are we ready yet to talk about that?

D: I don't mind waiting.

I: It's part of this process, too, isn't it?

D: I think so.

D: There are traces of magic surrounding the subjects, as if they were just returning from another realm. But also a rawness, in some cases, as though they'd been expelled from an enchanted place.

I: I don't know that they've been expelled. I have to believe they can return. It never occurred to me that my subjects were anything other than visitors.

D: Even in the photographs where there are no human forms, no fugitive shapes, ethereal wraiths, the work produces what I would call a combination of feelings in the viewer. That she has seen something so delicate and so fleeting, a shocking innocence. And that something or someone has just passed through the trees, however thick and shadowed. Or maybe a bird had just flown over and if one worked hard at it one could pick out the shadow of its flight from all the other shadows and mysteries of the forest.

I: You see, it's better these things come from you, than from me.

D: What spurred you on? Without an artistic community or critical reception of your work.

I: Part of the answer—only part, mind you—is that art can be made in isolated spots. With no hope or expectation of fame, in seclusion, without praise or critical acclaim. With very little notice at all. Art can be made to satisfy a curiosity, to follow a line of inquiry. Art, itself, can bear quite a lot, and it can be enough, or close to enough. There is above all a sacredness in creating something from nothing. I suppose in some ways, I wanted to be the proof of all this. Nor did I have a need to be discovered.

D: As I've "discovered" you.

I: Yes.

D: You've been here all along.

I: Exactly. But your intentions are what I'm interested in. They seem good. There are some who want to be known as much as they want the person they've unearthed to be known.

D: Shall we take a break now?

I: I need some tea. And let's have a dish of ice cream? I'm fond of Neapolitan.

[The tape is turned off and turned on again. There is silence for some time and then the sound of some assembling: papers being straightened, cups and plates being cleared, perhaps, moved aside.]

D: I couldn't do it. I couldn't make things without the hope that they'd become part of a conversation. I would need some notice. Regular praise, really.

I: But what does one give up for wanting that? Both states are imperfect. Do you ever imagine those who are creating all sorts of things, not so much in secrecy but hidden away, unconcerned? That is my community.

D: Do you think there are many undiscovered artists?

I: The thing to remember is that they wouldn't see themselves that way, as undiscovered artists. They're just making what they make.

I would play a section of the tape, and then rewind and play it again sentence by sentence as I transcribed.

I had set out to preserve Daphne's work when I began, as something you'd do for a friend, a talented and interesting friend, in memory. I had no expectation of it being anything grander than that. Yet, after the first 20 pages, it began to feel larger. I sensed they were working up to something, and even if that something was not revealed, I wanted to be in the presence of the secret. Or perhaps the taped conversations were a work of art unto themselves, and the listener found

herself in the unique position of being in the moment of creation every time they played. At times I wondered if the transcriptions were beside the point.

And then there were the notebooks as well, which I began to flip through, and then to delve into, at about this stage of listening to and transcribing the interviews. They were like the extras in a DVD of your favourite movie. They were like the composer's notes to a sublime piece of music. You didn't need to see them, and most people wouldn't want to, even. But I did.

She would jot things down and there would be lists, and then longer ruminations. Nothing was dated. A page might look like this:

How to ask a question.
What is at stake?

Today's interruptions: birdsong, someone at the door, the phone rings (we ignore it), vehicle drives in, gravel sounds, turns around, leaves.

A tape has been eaten and I've used a pencil to wind it back into the cassette, but the voices are garbled for a long stretch after that.

The cardigan Irene is wearing is beautiful. It's handmade, wool, cream, and the buttons are metal. I must remember to ask her who made it.

Irene is very fond of Neapolitan ice cream. She buys it in large pails and there are many empty pails on top of her fridge.

D: What was it that initially drew you to photography? And how did that change?
I: At first it was simply a form of meditation. I wanted to look more closely, to see things in detail. I began with

the pheasants, the goldens. Their wings and the configurations of their feathers. They are often described as secretive and nervous. And then I became entranced with the ring-necked pheasants, the way they rise up out of the brush, startled, and the trajectory of their flight. I wanted to catch the various angles, the low flight and the quiet as they rose. I kept coming back to the goldens. They've been diplomatically described as being more graceful on the ground than in the air. They've been kept as captive birds in Europe since the mid-eighteenth century and long before that in China, but little is known even now about their behaviour in the wild, in their natural habitat. I wanted to capture their awkward flying. The way they preferred not to fly, but to remain on the ground, even though they possess these beautiful wings. They're beautiful on the ground.

D: And this led you somewhere else.

Fra Angelico, *Annunciation*, 1442-43

I: What happens in making art, often, is that one is led. Something mundane, even, a small interest in one thing, will

carry you away to another. Or make you aware or tuned into a frequency to which previously you had not been attuned.

D: You've shown me your library.

I: I became interested in wings in art. I began with Fra Angelico.

I studied the colours of the wings, the palette. The shape of them. I didn't wonder whether the wings could achieve flight. I knew they could. Mostly, I just loved them. I found joy in looking at them.

D: Were you looking for something in particular?

I: Possibility. A way of seeing, a way of believing. I wasn't, I admit, looking at the wings through the lens of religion. I was looking at the angel as a messenger. We think we know what the message is in the scenes Fra Angelico painted. But that's making the message too small.

Fra Angelico, *Annunciation*, 1440-42

D: The colours of the wings are so beautiful. I could stare at them for a long time. The paintings are full of serenity. But also, the enormity is conveyed. Everything changes. A single point in time, one message, and then everything moves out from that.

I: I find myself identifying with both the messenger and the receiver of the message. I find myself asking with what gentleness is the message delivered? With what trepidation and awe is the message received? How does this scene play out in everyday life? Over and over. What responsibility to the world have we been given? How do we harbour it? Do we understand the gravity of the message? Do we understand our responsibility to the message? Do we understand our mission? Can we see the angel standing before us? Do we recognize the angel?

Albrecht Dürer, *Left Wing of a Blue Roller*

D: You were also looking at a particular Albrecht Dürer painting, the wing of a Blue Roller.

I: I was interested in how the bird wing was similar to but also quite different from Fra Angelico's angel wings. Of course, they were created 60 years apart.

D: Humans really are captivated by wings. I'm thinking about Da Vinci's drawings.

I: Oh yes, we could go on. Wings in art are plentiful. They occupy the collective imagination.

D: They have their own message.

I: I often wonder if I need to believe in God to believe in God. Do I need to believe in angels to believe in angels?

D: Maybe it's enough to receive. Maybe belief is merely receiving.

I: Grace.

D: We are in that space between keeping the secret and revealing the secret.

I: That space is the hallelujah.

D: The vestibule between knowing the secret and sharing the secret.

I: That is what it is right before the shutter is released. The eye sees. The finger depresses the button. There is the moment, the flash of time. And the image is captured. The time between seeing and capturing. The hangtime. That is for me a hallelujah.

D: And then the photograph itself emerges from the hallelujah.

I: And it occupies time and space. It moves through time as an object, a thin rectangle of light and darkness. It becomes a memory just as it becomes a thing. It clarifies and distorts an instant, simultaneously.

D: Maybe that is what an angel is. An angel is simultaneously the message. Simultaneously light and darkness. The annunciation of that.

I: That an angel need not be an angel. An angel need not have wings and wings need not be affixed to an angel.

D: Wings are a path just like any other path.

I: A photograph can be a message. It's a possible message. A possible annunciation.

D: The photograph might hang on by a thread.

I: The photograph exists as a time of approaching.

D: What is a poet but someone who approaches an un-gilded state? Golden no more.

I: There are moments when I have no expectations of anything happening. I give up on clicking the shutter. I can hear the nothingness in the air, I feel nothing. The miracle of being saved is not longed for. The miracle of something being revealed by my lens is clear. I'm clear. I have no hope, no expectations. I'm flying low. Then I know that I should take a photograph of myself.

D: A photograph can capture the secret of who a person is without ever revealing the secret. A photograph can hold the secrets a person has without telling them.

I: This is why it has been said that seeing is a miracle. And so, a photograph is a subset of that miracle. Something has been seen. And the seen is suspended.

D: I'm not a philosopher or a scholar of any sort. I don't know how to say so many of the things I want to hold.

I: Photographs can only take you into the realm. They are never the thing itself. This making of approximations, the photograph might approach the thing it captures, but it never really *is* that thing. It separates itself from what has been seen as soon as it exists as a thing. A flat surface.

D: The photograph is an illusion. A real illusion.

Xaviere

As I listened to Daphne and Irene, I began to form my own identity as an artist—as a poet. What is a poet? Someone who, in the act of becoming, allows herself to be written down.

I listened and then distanced myself from that listening. I tried to read these two lives as I might read a poem. How else was I to approach this task? I wasn't an archivist from the future, and these weren't some buried archives from the last century. Irene Guernsey wasn't completely unknown in her time. There'd been small shows, a couple of write-ups. She'd turned down speaking engagements, interviews.

There was an urge to go in and clean up the sentences, to explain this or that, to make her sound odder, or less odd. Because I didn't want the work diminished. And I needed to ask myself as I prepared and ordered: did this help the work or did it take away? Was it in service to the work? Did it strengthen the vibrations or spoil the mystery?

I suddenly wanted a photograph of the two of them together, talking, in Irene's living room. The entire time I was listening to the tapes, a picture formed in my mind. One of the walls would be wood-panelled, and the others are eggshell white. The couch that Irene sits on is floral, pinks and greens and oranges, and is in front of the pan- elled wall. Daphne sits on one of the two armchairs, across

from the couch, sometimes pulling her chair forward to be nearer to the tape machine on the coffee table between them. Sometimes she sits on her knees on the floor in front of the coffee table, so she can be nearer to Irene.

I knew that the first time they met, Irene had a large handbag at her feet as she sat on the couch, because Daphne had jotted this down in her journal. She described her: *She wears her long hair with strands of gray in a low ponytail. She has black-framed glasses, which she shoves on top of her head for the most part. A large silver bracelet. A black skirt and white shirt with a beautiful handmade wool sweater. The sweater is cream coloured with black metal buttons that seem to be Celtic knots.*

And I knew there was a painting on the wall above the couch, and that the painting wasn't centered over the couch but hung very low on the left side. So that when a person was sitting on the right side, it almost seemed as though there were two people.

The painting is of a young woman sitting on an armchair—sprawled on it, actually. She's holding a camera, a Rolleiflex camera. And she's glancing down so that we know she's seeing something across the room, through the window. The window is at an angle in the painting and so there is only a blurred image.

Why are we so interested in artists' studios? I wanted to know where Irene worked and what her darkroom was like. Still interesting, though less so, would be her house. I didn't necessarily want to know where she shot her photographs, but I did want to know what her daily perambulations might look like. I wanted a picture of her life, somehow. Which is made by noting one thing and not another. And so is not necessarily a clear picture but one that speaks nevertheless.

Listening to the conversations, I imagined a perfect solitude for Irene. A life of quiet and reclusiveness. Perhaps because Irene and Daphne talked solely about art and seeing and how an artist exists out of time. I never imagined Irene washing dishes or grocery shopping.

And I imagined what it must be like for Daphne after a session: perhaps she is sitting in her car. She drives down to the end of the long road from the lake to the highway and stops in at the old country store. She sits there for a while, jotting things in her notebook. For each day she visits Irene, she writes things down about the weather. She notes the rain on the windshield, or the snow she's brushed off the car. It's spring and she mentions how the lilac bushes have obliterated the old sign that said "Guernsey Pheasant Farm" beside the open gate of Irene's property. She mentions how pretty she thinks their empty ice cream dishes look on the coffee table, melted remains swirling in the bottoms of the crystal dishes. The chocolate and the strawberry and the vanilla merging.

I continued to transcribe, listening to the disembodied voices, typing sentence after sentence, slowly, for I'm no typist. I stopped and started the machine as I typed, praying the flimsy tape wouldn't jam or break. Sometimes I forgot to move my fingers over the keys and just listened, so that I had to rewind and find my place again.

When I looked back over the entire transcript of the 30 cassette tapes, the next moment seemed inevitable. What had been discussed up until this point had been merely a preamble. One could see that clearly afterwards. Suddenly we were knee deep in it, this experience of the numinous. To me, it felt like coming out of the fog into a meadow of dazzling light and bright green grass and wildflowers.

Irene and Daphne began that particular afternoon talking about books and pouring wine rather than the usual tea. Maybe that is why the talk seemed more fluid, the questions odder.

Daphne and Irene

Daphne: How is a photograph like a question?

Irene: Is a photograph like a question? Answers and questions are muddled… but maybe, no, what do you think?

D: Well, I've been thinking a lot about the nature of the question.

I: Of course you have.

D: What kinds of questions bring out what types of answers. And how a question is asked, the tone—is it gentle or probing or quiet, what is it trying to hide? The *how* is so important. But the intent is the thing, the integrity of the question.

I: The one asking tries to lead but is perhaps really only following. There is an attempt at a type of control. The one answering wonders at certain points if it would be wiser to be quiet. More measured. Less open, less giving. Or forthcoming.

D: If one asks a series of questions gently and then inserts a question that is less so, one that is rather more piercing. What happens then?

I: Yes.

D: It's not that I'm hiding anything, but when one speaks one truth, another is swept aside. And we haven't even spoken about memory.

I: It needs to be said how important the function of memory is to our seeing. There are so many layers that we bring to what we see and how we process those visions.

D: Why have you refrained from talking about your work until now? What changed your mind?

I: I've resisted because in the future it all might look foolish. Maybe the work will have disappeared. Or maybe it will seem irrelevant or simple. Why talk about work that doesn't last, for example? Who would want her words about her art to outlast her art?

But maybe most importantly, say the work does last—whatever I say will sound presumptuous. And I don't want my words to become part of the work. I don't want to be quoted; I want the work to inhabit space, alone. Pictures should, you know.

D: But you want people to understand it?

I: Yes, but on their own terms without my intervention.

D: And if they misinterpret it because of your silence?

I: Then that is their misinterpretation. Just as perhaps I misinterpreted what I saw and then proceeded to coax this mis-seeing onto the photo paper.

D: Was there something you persisted in hoping to see?

I: I had seen something. And then disbelieved my own seeing. It wasn't so much that I was hoping to see it, but that I wished to revisit the seeing. I wanted to understand my seeing. I wanted to take my seeing for a long walk and I wanted it to come to me as a foal in a large paddock comes to its first human hand: gently and carefully, but with innocence and willed trust.

D: And did the foal come to you?

I: I began to understand the work was fated, from here on in. No matter what I had seen or thought I had seen, my seeing changed my course.

D: And the foal? Your seeing?

I: Yes.

[Pause. There is the sound of someone moving back and forth in her chair. What sounds like breathing. Silence. And then a different sort of silence.]

I: I had begun by taking photos of the air after a bird had flown by. A ring-necked pheasant would burst up out of the grass, and I would photograph that wild eruption into the sky. But what I was really interested in was the air after the bird had flown off. The disruption in air after flight. The trees and scrub around where the bird had taken off. So there are a lot of photos where it might seem as though nothing is happening in them. An emptiness. But they're photos of the moment after, of air at a different frequency, air that has altered, been stirred up and full, and then suddenly emptied.

The goldens make half-hearted attempts to fly as though they know something. Once in a while there would be some energetic lifting off, so colourful. But their wings are short and their tails long, and they are not designed for the open air.

D: There are photos of colourful blurs, wingtips, the tops of willow trees, and then after these photographs you move to capturing birds in flight, often very far away. Specks in the sky. Or geese flying very low.

I: And this went on for a very long time. It's important to note. This particular body of work isn't extensive because I kept only very select photos that captured the feeling, the phenomenon, I was searching for. Hunting, stalking it, waiting and waiting. There is so much waiting and quiet around this series of photographs. And only so many in the end were worthy. I would be out waiting and only depress the shutter once in a period of two weeks, say. And I say that I was hunting for these images, but they were seeking me.

D: The viewer feels this of course. A vastness. A tremulousness. The air is quaking, so still, so full.

I: Right, right.

I also want to say that I know anyone could have taken these photographs. Anyone who happened to be where I was,

who was open to seeing, who had a camera. Any type of camera. I think that needs to be said.

D: Alright. That's good.

There is silence for a couple of minutes, a longer interval than usual.

D: A little more?

[The sound of wine being poured. Another interval where they each take a sip. A sigh, and the glasses are put on the table. The sigh sounds like satisfaction.]

I: And then came the children.

D: Heavens, yes.

I: And then came the children, flying through the forest. Which reminded me a little of the goldens, you see. They'd adapted, as a species, to being bound to the forest floor, wings too small. Short flights, but colourful ones.

D: You're speaking metaphorically.

I: I'm speaking…

D: Yes, yes.

I: Right.

D: And then there are the girls with long hair who are standing on stumps in the trees. They're positioned so that branches appear to be erupting from their backs. A camera trick, but very effective.

I: Is it?

D: Is it what?

I: A trick?

D: The light in that same photo is ethereal. Very misty and full. I want to say magical.

I: You can, you know. Say magical. It's not the only thing the photo strives for but it's something.

D: Magical is too light of a word, I sometimes think. Or is it that it's overused?

I: I agree. Though it's as close as we can get to naming certain ineffable moments. One summer day, there was a girl wearing a white party dress, which was unusual. Attire was very casual by the lake. She had a navy-blue one-piece bathing suit on underneath and she'd likely put on this party dress without her mother knowing and ran outdoors on her way to the beach. But something stopped her in the little clearing I'd grown fond of and she began to twirl. I'd been photographing birds in birch trees a ways off, but the clearing was always in the back of my mind, you see. And when she appeared and twirled then stopped, I thought, well, you've missed it. But she began again, as though commanded to do so, not by me, but by some unknown force or forces. I took numerous photos.

D: But you narrowed it down to one.

I: Oh yes, you have to keep going until you've found the one that says the most, feels the most. Which is a very difficult part of the process. You don't always know which one it is when you're taking the photos.

D: But did you with this one?

I: Yes.

I: Yes.

D: What happened when you found it afterwards? When it appeared in the darkroom?

I: The whole time I was shooting, I knew it would appear. The special something, but I didn't know what that would be, precisely.

D: I don't know that I'm asking the right questions.

I: Do you want me to say what it was?

D: Not yet. Not really, unless you want to say.

I: I do, actually. I didn't think I would.

D: Okay.

I: I'll simply say, wings. Let's call them angel wings.

D: They were there in that one photo.

I: They were there, and not there in the others.

D: Did you doubt what you were seeing?

I: Not for a second.

D: But they're not there in the other photos?

I: Not at all.

D: Could they have been the effect of the dress and the trees and the motion?

I: No. No. I don't see how.

D: Okay, okay.

[Here there is a silence. Then what may have been a spoon dropping into an ice cream dish.]

D: Can you describe the image?

I: It's difficult.

D: Yes.

I: But it's there. You could see it? There are some who couldn't when it was shown. It was as if what I saw, and others could see, was invisible to some viewers. This was the most fascinating thing.

D: Oh yes, and even though the image is in black and white, I could see the colours. I could taste them; I could taste the colours as I saw them.

I: That makes sense to me. Tell me what you tasted.

D: A dark red cherry, a fresh mint, the yellow was very caramel-y. And there was a vanilla custard in very small amounts. Blue was unexpected. Not blueberry, but something sophisticated, more like a salty caviar on a cream cracker. But you know, I was a child really, when I saw your photographs in that exhibition. My parents had taken me, they were always dragging me into galleries, but I don't really remember looking at what was on the wall (though I must have at least tried) until this show of yours.

D: After this photo there is a space in your work, which you always dated. A silence.

I: Maybe what's interesting is how, at this point, when I look back at the images I've made, when I think about them, time just collapses, and it is as though everything I made, all the photographs, are just one continuous book. Folded one into the next. As though there are no spaces, no time between them. But of course, there was so much waiting. There were silences. There were times I was desperate to see something, to make art, to take a photograph. It's not as though I don't remember the lulls, the torture, even, of them. I do. But in the end, one edits them out little by little—our memory does that.

D: If you could go back in time and talk to yourself…

I: Yes, every artist wishes that—just that we could go back and whisper in our own ear: continue, continue…

D: Have courage.

I: Just so.

D: What else would you say?

I: Persist. Persist, persist, persist.

I: And then I would say that we waste too much time, we artists, doubting. We lose our nerve. I would say, you can still work when you have lost your nerve. Keep working through the lack of courage and the loss of nerve and the despair. If you are an artist, if you have been called, this is your obligation. Imagine that everything you make is part of a huge book, some big Anselm Kiefer-like book that fills half a room and opens up like angel wings. And that if you stop, even for a while, you've robbed the readers of a page or a chapter. Even if it's a poor chapter, they will want to see it because it's part of the whole, you see.

D: That's a beautiful way of putting it.

[A pause, some settling-in sounds.]

D: I wonder if you'd like to talk about what did drive you. The force behind your instinct to keep pushing forward.

What kept you wanting to frame things, to capture the light? In short, why did you persist?

I: Well, to begin with, I had enough money. Not too much, so that I wasn't tempted by other things. But I knew if I managed what I had, I could go on. So. I had that. This is never talked about enough.

But I also had this abiding love, which comes from nowhere, this abiding love for making pictures, finding light, finding humans in a certain light, animals, things. But mainly humans. One becomes a disciple of light, and of the mysteries of the rectangle, you know. The mystery of what one finds in that particular frame. And you know, I read somewhere, "seeing is a miracle." And I can't emphasize that enough. Knowing that, understanding it repeatedly, and then to learn it each time one has a successful photo arrive. That kept me chasing my light—my angels, as it were.

D: I love what you said there: that you had become a *disciple of light*…

I: I really felt that I was.

D: I just need to jot that down in my notebook, too…

I: Okay, go ahead.

D. Okay. And, *seeing is a miracle.*

[There is a pause and a rustle of a bag, the notebook being extracted from the bag, another faraway thin sound which must be the act of writing, and then a soft thump as the notebook is set on the table.]

D: Okay. Thank you.

I: You're welcome.

D: It's sometimes difficult for non-artists to understand what makes a good photograph. To develop a discernment. To go far enough into looking.

I: Yes. This will always be the case. What people need to know about looking at a photograph is that you are likely

to meet the photographer there if you swim out, swim into it. If you learn to breathe with the strokes of the swimming. I draw light into me through the camera, through the held breath. The particular breathing of a photographer, yes? Very like a swimmer, timing breaths with each stroke, each surfacing. Does that help, do you think?

D: Well, no. No, but it's beautiful.

[They both laugh.]

D: Maybe we should stop here for the day.
I: I'm a little tired, yes.
You're back tomorrow.
D: If you'll have me.
I: I will.

D: After the moment of the girl in the forest, that summer there was a short series of still lifes. Feathers. Very profound, singular.

Daphne wrote in her journal: *When I walk in, she's sitting, she's holding a book to her chest and later when we sit, tea on the table before us, the tape recorder beside the tea tray*.................

I: I began to imagine I was just seeing what I had studied, or some fantasy of it.
D: We go further along in your oeuvre and find these. Let me show you something. This would be the winter following the summer of the twirling girl with wings. [Digs in book bag.]
I have photographs of my mother and father and me, at an installation of your work at a small gallery. Part of a small group show. I would have been the same age as some of the children you photographed. I remember the exhibit very clearly. It was Narnian, for me. As though I'd stepped

through the back of the wardrobe and come out in another land steeped in magic.

I: Oh yes, I remember that show. My work was minimized, really, you know.

D: Well, it was in a small room at the back of the gallery.

I: And hardly anyone thought to go there. Unless they were invited.

D: But it was a perfect discovery for a small child.

I: I really was drawn to the room. No one invited me, I just knew I had to go. The walls were painted white and the photographs did suit the room.

D: My parents took these photographs of me looking at your photographs! I guess I didn't want to leave and they thought it was sweet. I felt as though that room were Narnia, I really did.

I: The snow.

D: Well, yes, the snow, but more so, the magic.

I: What did you feel?

D: I was going to ask you the same thing.

I: They're attracted to recently abandoned snow angels of children.

D: The angels?

I: Yes. Yes, the angels.

D: That's an astonishing thing to say.

[Silence.]

I: Yes, I know.

D: I feel like I'm entering a children's book again, just talking to you.

I: In winter they're even more apparent, and they like those picturesque days, fresh and sparkling snow, lightly falling snow, the big flakes. But this makes it difficult to photograph them.

D: Are they quite white, quite light?

I: Are they pure light?

D: Are they?

I: I think that's the answer. But they were also very colourful. Like Durer's wings.

D: The photographs are black and white, but you know I read them as colour, I saw them in colour. In the snapshots my parents took, you can see that I'm in colour and the photographs are in black and white. But I remember them in colour. I have always felt confused looking through my family album.

[A long silence.]

D: Let's talk more about the images, the photographs.

I: I'd like that. Sometimes I think back to this particular series. Often, in truth. So I start thinking about the feeling taking the photos, which was like falling back into a deep snow bank. And then about processing them. And then showing them, framing them and showing them. The way that the photos then take over the experience, one's memory of actually shooting them, but not as much as is usually the case, because when I was taking the photos—that was such a powerful moment.

D: I remember the photo of the children rising up out of their snow angels, amid the trees. The snow sparkles and even thought the photo is black and white—as I said, I see it in my mind's eye in colour. The blue cast of the snow, the bright colours of their jackets and hats. And then they leave and there's another photo of them going away. And lastly we come to the rest of the photos that are the magical ones.

I: That word again. [They laugh together.] But, yes.

D: The photographs are good because they see for us, they tell us what might sound strange in words.

I: And not everyone sees what I think you see in the photo, what I see also.

D: This to me was part of the magic—my parents didn't see the angels rising out of the snow angels after the children had left.

I: Those who see them have trouble pointing them out to those who can't.

D: My parents thought I was being very imaginative. They shook their heads, saying, "It's a trick of the eye." They listened to me and I think wanted to see but couldn't. I remember them trying. But I knew what I was seeing, and I was lost in it, transported. It's never happened quite like that before or since.

I: How did you make sense of it?

D: I just accepted it.

I: Yes.

D: So there were five or six large photographs in the room, and to a child they seemed very large, so that I felt I could leave the room behind. I could walk right into the images, because they were bigger than I was.

I: It was important that I print them as large as possible.

D: The viewer is on the threshold. When I began to read the C.S. Lewis book, I remember feeling as though I were going into the wardrobe with the children but that after that, I watched them in Narnia from a distance, from the threshold. I was reading from the threshold place. It was like that. The moment when you are in the wardrobe but can see this other place.

I: Yes, go on.

D: I'm looking at the photographs, and I'm almost in them, but I know I can't continue; I can only peer in from my vantage point, from the threshold. But still, I'm transfixed. I'm filled with wonder and joy. I remember that feeling so well.

I wanted the feeling to last as long as possible, so I kept looking and looking. And I saw the snow angels, and the trees and the softly falling flakes. The photos were so detailed that I could see individual snowflakes and the bark of the birch trees. The scruff of the tree and the papery bark. I could see the creases of the children's jackets and ski pants left in the snow angels.

I: It's amazing what the camera can record.

D: These winged creatures were trying to do something, to say something. Did they speak to you?

I: You mean other than metaphorically? Did they literally speak to me? No. But messages aren't always spoken or transmitted per se. They're given as images that sink into us over time. And honestly, it took a while. I tried to just take the photographs and not think about what was happening.

D: What would you say was happening? What was the message?

I: The message…

D: Yes, yes.

I: For a while I thought the message had to do with the end of things. I did.

D: How? Why? Really?

I: It takes a while for messages, the ones that come this way, to make sense. One needs to internalize the images, the feelings.

[The sound of a spoon in a crystal dish. I imagine it might be from a dish of Neapolitan ice cream.]

D: What are angels?

I: Yes.

D: Shall we talk about angels?

I: I think we have to.

D: Have you watched the movie *Wings of Desire*?

I: Yes, I did. But. It was after everything.

D: And is it something like that? The scene in the library, the angels helping people, they're invisible, guiding. A child can see them. But no one else does.

I: It's not completely unlike that. Less ominous though. They were visible to me. They seemed to both have form and also be formless. Or that they could go back and forth. But in the movie, they had no wings, and this is really what I was focused on, these beautiful wings.

D: They're blurry but they're defined.

I: They're almost nonexistent. Like the skeletons of leaves that you might find at the end of winter.

D: Very white, translucent. But the wings are also colourful in some shots, or one imagines them as such. Did you wish you'd used colour film?

I: I know it's not logical, but I don't think it would have worked.

D: I remember you once talking about the sound of wings. How your life has been lived to the sound of wings. Did that come out of this moment, or was it from before?

I: This is when I realized what I had been hearing. It had been there all along. So many things that perplex us in life are like this. We are on the cusp of understanding. We know things without knowing them. Or we know them before we know them.

D: Which is why it's important to listen to our inner leanings...

I: If I had, well. The thing is that truths—deep personal truths, and the large universal ones, too—they come up slowly, they rise in us, so that we may feel the fullness and wholeness of them.

D: Yes, yes.

I: And the wonderful, wonderful thing about recording the moment, even if the images don't deliver the same message to everyone who views them, is that I can use it to remember. It's proof, even for just me.

D: We could stop here for today.

I: Let's turn off the tape and have a cookie together or a dish of ice cream. The tea is cold. I'll boil new water.

[Rustling sounds, the tape being turned off.]

Daphne: Where should we start today?
Irene: Oh, anywhere.
D: Are you sure?

[Silence, papers being shuffled, the sound of someone readjusting their seating, a sniff, a throat being cleared.]

D: Let's start slowly. What I've been wondering is, would things have been different if you'd become famous? We were talking last time about what I think of as your Narnia show. It was in the back room of a larger gallery. Easy to overlook, though not everyone did. I'm proof of that.

I: What would fame have even looked like then? Fame wasn't even a remote possibility for me, because of where I lived. Because of the time. Shows came and went so quickly. There were some reviews but not many. And often the reviews were written by some young art student or recent graduate with an art history degree who had never traveled or seen much art. There were catalogues raisonnés, invitation cards. But, from here, things didn't make the national newspaper very often, or even the local newspaper. Even the artists who were well known in this area weren't known in other parts of the country.

D: So you weren't invited to speak or lecture at the university? You weren't invited to fancy dinner parties?

I: Oh heavens, that's amusing to contemplate, but no. Certainly not. I wouldn't have dreamt of such things, though, either.

D: Why?

I: The work had to keep its secrets.

D: You're thinking about belief?

I: I'm thinking about how we've learned to keep ourselves at a distance from mystery. In the everyday. We're cut off from our dream life, perhaps, from entire ways of thinking about the world, our existence. But let me say, if I'd had some attention, things would have been different. Attention can be both good and bad for one's creative endeavours, shall we say. We tell ourselves that it has to not matter, because the work is the important thing, though we know it does matter. It matters. At the same time, it's such joyous freedom to work

anonymously, quietly, going deeper and deeper into the work alone. There is no doubt in my mind that my work had a greater clarity because there were so few outside distractions.

D: What else is your work about, would you say?

I: Solitude.

D: Solitude?

I: We who are alone, we see things differently. We experience things in a different way than those who go home after their work to a loved one. I've always thought that this is the great consolation of being alone. At the start, when I photographed the children, most often when they were alone in the woods, running or playing, once in a while just musing, they were usually alone. Certainly alone in their thoughts in the way that only children can be. I was alone with my thoughts a great deal. The children were there, I came to think, to firmly believe, to alert me to the presence of angels among us. Beginnings. What I noticed was that some of the children, who had begun with small wings one summer, would come back the next without them. And for others, the wings had grown more pronounced. Maybe they weren't children at all. I don't know.

I felt I was being led, though. It feels like that mostly afterwards, looking back, but the feeling was there to a lesser degree all along. At the time I was shaken; I didn't know why I was the one seeing what I saw. Part of me wanted to ignore it, move, put my camera way. For a time I drank. Tall crystal glasses of very cold tonic and too much gin. I'd put my glass in the freezer, then add ice, the gin, and a splash of tonic.

D: This is understandable.

I: Is it?

I was in need of the sort of clarity that one only finds at the bottom of a bottle of gin. If you want to reach the extremities of your soul, that's one way. It's not the only way, but it can be a quick route. In a way I knew my photographs had to speak across this abyss, to someone else who has been cleansed by this horrible intelligibility. The genius of the

drunk. It's not a state to be proud of, I don't recommend it, because it's also a kind of hell in the wrong body, but it can be necessary. It can be sublime. It can echo a certain state, a truly profound state.

D: People think that drinking can cloud things, but it can also focus.

I: The focus at a certain point in one's drinking is absolute.

D: No distractions.

I: What people don't understand is how empowering that state is, potentially.

[Laughter.]

D: But you stopped. Maybe you had your own guardian angel.

I: Well.

D: You haven't stopped?

I: I will never stop drinking. I'm too old now to stop. My body would rebel. And it's the only way I can get back to where I was.

D: This is important.

I: Yes.

D: What have you seen that surprised you? Or was it all a surprise?

I: Seeing is like that—one persists in going out with a camera because one expects, hopes, to be surprised. At the same time one knows the unlikelihood. But what surprised me, what surprises me now, is how when I was young, I wanted to be known, really felt and understood and known, through my art. If the viewer could really look deeply into my photographs, then they were also looking deeply into me. I needed this. Never got it.

D: Okay.

I: And in my older age, which happened early for me, you could say. I left my youth behind early, ages ago. I left

that behind. That's one of the gifts of following through with one's art—never giving up, carrying on and never letting up.

D: There are other things that surprised you, too.

I: Oh yes, oh yes.

D: Mmmhmm.

I: You'll enjoy this. And it doesn't matter if you believe it. It seems obvious to me and has since I witnessed it, but angels turn into birds occasionally.

D: Oh, really. Okay.

I: You'd never imagined this?

D: Not at all. I really hadn't, but it sort of makes sense, doesn't it?

I: I think so.

D: It would be in the blink of an eye. So you'd question it. Dismiss it.

I: Exactly.

D: What else?

I: That angels are complicated and sometimes deliver harsh messages. That they are among us, but also arrive. There are guardian angels, but there are more complicated angels too. Often one and the same. I'm not an expert, you see. I never strived to be so. I never once went looking in this way. I just went, open.

D: Did you ever want to turn away? Leave your subject matter behind? Go elsewhere?

I: I had the impression that it would follow me. Maybe not exactly as it was, but in some other iteration. I really did. I don't think we choose our subject matter.

D: Why do you think they kept arriving? Or revealing themselves to you?

I: At first, I thought it was related to inspiration, that particular state of grace. The very breath of my creativity conjured them. I began to wonder very quickly if I might not even understand what it is to be in a state of grace. What is meant by that.

D: This was short lived.

I: The idea that I knew anything dissipated quite quickly. That I was special in any way. These weren't useful things, anyway. I had to get out of the way of the work because it wasn't about me. This was actually a very liberating revelation for me.

[The sound of one of the women standing, probably Irene. Steps away and then back after a short wait. Something is set down.]

D: Did you ever feel as though you were becoming unbalanced? What did all this visual information you were witnessing and recording do to you?
I: This is well put. This is very well put. Thank you.

[Paper rustling.]

I: Somehow, I tricked my mind into thinking that what I was seeing was metaphorical. That though I believed what I was seeing, it had the same value as reading a story, like the Marquez story, do you know it?
D: I don't. I'll look it up.
I: It's titled "A Very Old Man with Enormous Wings: A Tale for Children."
D: Is it? A tale for children?
I: Oh, no, I don't think so. A tale for adults who have retained something of the children they were. Having said that, I don't know who it's for. It's for rare individuals, I suppose.
What I was seeing could exist in the same realm as the story.
D: It could be accepted.
I: It's amazing what the mind will accept.
D: So one part of your mind understands what you're seeing as a kind of metaphor. For what?
I: This is what needs working out and changes with various readings. Is it that the angel is standing in for something, coming to fill that void we all have?

D: It's an emptiness.

I: Precisely.

D: So in your next show, after your Narnia show, there was an angel who seemed to be hiding in each of the frames. Either just in the frame or walking out of it. Disappearing into the trees. But in the catalogue essay for the show, the angel isn't even mentioned.

I: I know.

D: This seemed strange to me.

I: It was. Yes. Strange.

D: But in a way this had to be.

I: Entirely. If the angel had been mentioned…

D: It would have taken away from the experience of the viewer.

I: Right.

D: The viewer comes to see the photographs with no expectations really, just to see some eerie forest pictures maybe. And then slowly, the angel reveals himself. But not to everyone.

Xaviere

As I was writing down their words, I felt as though I were part of that dialogue. I was becoming part of it. Their words were becoming part of me, in the same way that a dream re-told several times becomes a memory. It becomes real in that way.

This insane gift of two women talking. So commonplace and yet so elusive. Like birds singing to each other in a stand of trees—it's hard to find the one singing, and then one off in another tree responds. You spot one and the song comes from another place.

What was interesting to me was thinking about how the words, these two voices, the two women, answering and questioning and listening and breathing together in a room, believing in each other—how that was life changing. Perhaps for them, but certainly for me, listening in later. The genuine interest in the asking, the generosity in the act of answering. How beautiful this was, how delightful.

What more do you need to know other than: there were two women in a room together one winter. One woman asked questions and recorded another woman's answers.

There is the poetry of silence and the poetry of talking. The poetry of the tape playing sounds of silence and rustling and breathing and existing in the same space.

What does it mean when two women get together and hold a conversation, when they get to that point where only honesty

comes into play? What is honesty when we are talking to one another? How do we sidestep and hover and falter? What happens when in a conversation there is no hiding or concealing but just a very concerted effort to get at the heart of things? A conversation like that can take an unexpected turn. How does the listener take in this information but still keep moving forward in the conversation? How to keep up?

And then, one wonders, what is at stake here? Why is it important to recover their words, to listen in, to record? Is the desire to capture what would otherwise be lost, the ephemeral, enough? Is it a worthwhile pursuit to try to preserve the revelations of an instant, two minds thinking together, two women thinking aloud and breathing together and wondering and believing together?

What is the point of recording a conversation that doesn't change the world or make it better in some tangible way? If it doesn't move things and thought forward? A gentle conversation, the back and forth, the quiet thinking, the calm interchange—where is the place for that in this world? Are we really responsible for each other? Can we say it has to do with degrees? But what kind of responsibility is that? We are either responsible or we are not. Can a conversation deepen our responsibility to another? Can it underline the importance of one human being to another?

There was an openness, and I didn't use the word "open" lightly. When we are open there is a vulnerability that is so fragile and dangerous. We can be destroyed in that stance.

The words in this conversation became feathers, and the sentences became wings. I felt that they were very close to becoming enormous wings. They were flying low, these women, but it was quite possible that they would take flight and rise high into the sky with their great wings. Listening, I knew that they didn't know this themselves, but I could hear it in the frequencies of the silences in the tape recording. It was building, the air was trembling, and it was powerful and wonderfully terrifying.

Daphne and Irene

D: You wanted to begin today talking about the angel.

I: Yes.

D: Okay.

I: He arrived at the very end of fall; there was already snow on the ground and it stayed, which made it a particularly long winter that year. He became known as the winter pheasant, because no one wanted to say the word angel. When he arrived, it was still hunting season, and when I first came upon him, he seemed wounded. He was always trying to hide his left shoulder.

He looked like one of Michelangelo's figures from the Sistine chapel. The ones holding up things. He was muscular in an otherworldly way.

Maybe he had been meant for another destination or dimension because he wasn't dressed for winter and he seemed to dislike it at first. People brought clothes and knitted things. So that in a few weeks he was looking like a sort of yarn-bombed angel.

D: Didn't anyone ask the angel questions?

I: People didn't know what they were seeing. Many thought it was some sort of joke, or entertainment, that maybe he was going to be part of some movie. So then, those who came to see, they took up a role for themselves—sceptic,

joker, quiet observer. Many were just quiet. Some cried, some believed. Some felt they knew the angel or that they had met him before. But rarely did anyone attempt to talk to the angel. Maybe because of the sighs.

D: Oh?

I: He would sigh and make guttural noises, unearthly loud, drowning out any other noise or talking. He was in pain, this was obvious, but the sounds also seemed to indicate some kind of psychic pain, as well. I wondered if he was calling out, calling for help. I'm not sure. Who would hear him? Would the other angels hear him?

[The sound of the tape coming to an end.]

D: When the tape ran out, you mentioned poetry.

I: A few people brought books from the library. One older gentleman who used to be an English professor brought a small stool and sat outside the cage and read poetry. I remember him reading the Milosz poem about angels that begins, "All was taken away from you: white dresses / wings, even existence. / Yet I believe you, / messengers." He came back a few times, the professor.

D: That's lovely. But how did the angel react? And had he been wearing white?

I: When he arrived, he was wearing something like a white nightgown—multiple gowns it seemed, one on top of the other, a great many of them—but because it was so cold, he'd wrapped the inner layers around his legs and made a cape out of others. Maybe he'd even used some to bandage his shoulder, or to take the weight off of it. I think there was a sling for a while. I should say that it was the most incredible fabric. Beautifully textured, embossed, embroidered in places with a curious design.

D: You touched it?

I: Oh, yes.

D: And he didn't mind you touching him?

I: I think the pain changed his normal demeanour. He allowed what he wouldn't have allowed, what no one would have dared had he been at full strength. It was less that he minded, but that it was a new circumstance, something he'd not experienced. Something I'd not experienced. New territory.

D: And those who came, they just stood and stared?

I: Yes, there were a few short stools that people had brought. They would sit and stand. Grow restless. But they looked at him as though he were a painting in a museum, or a lion at the zoo. Absorbed, a bit wary, ultimately restless. It was cold, too, that winter, so very few stayed for long intervals. No one for more than an hour. Once in a while a feather would find its way out of the pheasant cage and I'd see someone pocketing it.

D: He stayed in the pheasant coop all winter?

I: Yes. At first, he cowered in the corner and refused to be led into the house. I tried. Eventually, I dragged out an old army cot that was in the house. I piled blankets on top of it. He ignored the cot for weeks. And then one day it was all set up, and one of the sheets hanging from the ceiling was over it. Later, when he was slightly better, when I was out, he must have come into the house and taken a lamp. There was electricity out there. He'd also found magazines. *Ladies' Home Journal* and *People* magazine. And he used a bit of mud and stuck pages of them to the back of the cage. Which was a large cage—it had been for the goldens, remember.

D: So he made this cage a kind of home?

I: For a while. But when no one was around he'd wander. Not very far at first, but then he'd disappear for twenty minutes, then thirty, and then for up to an hour or two.

D: What do you think he was doing?

I: I had the feeling that he was looking for something.

D: And his wing?

I: He hid it, favoured it, I think you could say. It drooped. He hid them both, or tried to, but they were enormous, so

it was impossible. He hid them as a child sometimes tries to hide by closing their eyes.

D: Everyone wanted to see the wings.

I: Yes, but what was interesting was that there were those who couldn't see them. It's just an old man, a homeless man, I heard some say, but they didn't ask for their money back, either, which they had given without my asking. I saved it for him. I overheard long discussions about belief. And I sometimes caught a person throwing things at him, lobbing small stones. They didn't hurt him, but all the same, I put a stop to that. Of course, it worked, especially one time, early on, when a man tossed a pebble and it hit him on the shoulder, his wounded shoulder. The angel half-rose from his seated position on the cot, where he'd been assuming the pose of Rodin's *Thinker*. He forgot to hide his wings and they appeared, suddenly, the one drooping, the other massive and impressive. And just as quickly, he remembered, and they were furled, tucked. Still, it was indelible, that scene.

D: You were photographing him, all through this.

I: I wasn't sure if I should. Quite honestly, it didn't seem right. But then, I was compelled to do so. I thought, I'll take the photos, but no one has to see them. What I found shocking was that no one who came to visit the angel brought any camera equipment at all. Some people did sketch him. But no one snapped photos that I knew of, and I was attentive to this. I don't think I would have stopped it, since he didn't seem to mind, but it never happened.

D: You showed me earlier a single photograph. Would you describe it for the tape?

I: It was of this moment, though not terribly well captured. I was about to chastise the man who'd lobbed the pebble. I'd seen him pick it up out of the corner of my eye but didn't really believe he'd throw it. So, I'd lowered the camera to my chest. When the angel's wings emerged, it was a whirlwind, and I just snapped and manually advanced the film, then took one more snap, and in that span of time, it was

over. So the image is blurred, but I think maybe that's what makes it interesting and real.

D: Let's go back to the sounds he made.

I: Soon he began to speak. But he didn't speak in English. Some people told me they'd had the most amazing thoughts or ideas, in his vicinity. Some even requested a pen and paper to write them down. One woman told me she'd had all these thoughts and feelings, but that they left her as soon as she'd moved away from the cage. It was like remembering dreams, she said, that elusive, that haunting.

D: A lot of people came?

I: Word got out somehow. And for a while there were line-ups. On Sunday, the road in front of the house would be lined with cars. I wouldn't let them in the driveway – I left the big metal gate closed and there was a chain and lock around it, as is the custom on the road to the lake. I was afraid they'd get stuck in the snow or just want to stay. So I opened the smaller side gate and they started giving me money.

D: Yes, you'd mentioned there were payments.

I: I never said I wanted money, but it just became the norm. Twenty dollars each. It was understood, somehow, though I wasn't the one to set the rate. I'm not sure where the sum came from. But I had a box, and I just kept taking what people silently gave. I tried to refuse a couple of times. I wasn't sure what they were paying for or what they thought they'd get for their money. In the end, I realized most of them just wanted to be in the presence of the angel. No one ever asked for their money back, anyway. And I imagined I might need it to help him someday, I wasn't sure how.

D: Of course.

I: I think I'm forgetting to say things. Where I first came across the angel. In the woods. Near where the snow angels were, you see.

D: That makes sense.

I: Though nothing to do with the angels really, of course. He seemed to be of a very different ilk, anyway. Not that I'm

any expert whatever. Maybe their appearance was meant as some sort of practice for me, or maybe, I think this is true, maybe it was just a coincidence.

[They sip tea; a clatter of cups.]

I: First I found a heap of feathers, below a tree.

D: What did they look like?

I: The first ones I found were beautiful and very small. Fledgling feathers. Soft and downy around the bottom and edges. They fit in the palms of my hands and I couldn't stop looking at them. I took them home right away; they were so precious.

D: You found more.

I: I went back a couple of days later and there were more. A disturbing amount, larger. But, oh, so beautiful! They took my breath away.

D: You collected them?

I: I did. They were exquisite. The colours were like nothing I'd seen. I still can hardly believe I held them in my hands.

D: And did you photograph them then?

I: I didn't. I was just walking and, unusual for me, I didn't take my camera. For some reason it didn't occur to me to photograph them where I'd found them. The next day, I took my camera and there were more feathers. I took one photograph, but there was something wrong with the film, and the sun was so bright. I don't know exactly what happened, but the subject is difficult to discern in the snow. It was as though there had been an intervention.

D: So there were all these feathers. And you collected them.

I: It seemed wrong to leave them there, these moultings, these bedraggled cast-offs. I filled the pockets of my old canvas coat. But as I was standing there, a feather floated down, one and then another, from the sky, through the trees. I have since sometimes thought that we should all walk around

with our hands out, cupped a little, ready to receive what falls from the sky.

[There is a pause. A quiet. Only the sound of the tape.]

I: I looked up. One is compelled to when something so beautiful floats down before your eyes, and lands so softly on the early snow of winter. I looked up, and the angel was there. And it seemed inevitable. It made sense.

D: The angel was there, where?

I: Not floating mid-air. I was almost expecting that, if I was expecting anything. A hovering. But no, the angel was wounded and was hunched over, perched on an old hunter's blind. A small platform up in the trees. Luckily it wasn't terribly high. And somehow, I coaxed him down. I showed him the feathers and he nodded and I picked the few remaining ones up and he nodded again. And then he made his way down the makeshift ladder – just small boards nailed onto the tree. Very precarious. It was frightening watching him descend. I was worried he'd fall and I wouldn't know at all what to do with him then. But he made it. He descended slowly and I could tell he was in pain; he seemed delirious. With every rung downward, an involuntary anguished sound, a sort of song, a whistling, but filled with agony. And even though I knew the sound was an eruption of pain, I couldn't help but be mesmerized by the beauty of the utterance—so pure and otherworldly, so full. The sound happened in layers and layers, piercing and heavenly, and seemed to go on forever until it stopped. One searches for words and cannot find them. But the experience had the effect of combining senses, so it was like melted chocolate and the scent after rain and then deep cello sounds, all mixed together in a sensory experience. I found it amazing that this sound was a manifestation of pain, and yet one knew it was.

D: Did it hurt to hear?

I: In a certain way, yes. But it also created a very deep empathy, instantly, though I couldn't have named the emotion when I was feeling it.

D: Why do you think the angel came? Why was he here?

I: I started with the feeling that he'd been blown off course. As I said, he didn't seem properly attired for our winter climate. But did I expect an angel to arrive in a parka? Why do angels arrive at all? Are they here to act as guardians? To announce a death? An angel of witness? A messenger? Was he really an angel? Well, I ask all these questions now, but when I walked him toward my house, through the trees, slowly in the deeper snow, and then onto worn paths, him leaning on me, I didn't have questions. I only wanted to get him where he could heal. I only wanted to help relieve his pain.

D: You felt this as an obligation?

I: I would say it was deeper than that. I felt an absolute need.

D: I know I should be asking more philosophical questions, more esoteric ones. But it's the physical situation that I'm so intrigued by, that I feel I need to know more about, first. I mean, how do you entertain an angel? What do you feed him?

I: These were concerns. But I was led by the angel even when I thought otherwise. I tried to take him into the house but he went straight to the golden pheasant pen. I protested, but this was to no avail. It was a relief when he accepted the cot, as I mentioned earlier. I tried a lot of food, but what he liked, what he would eat, was whipped cream and cereal.

D: Boxed cereal?

I: Dry cereal. Fruit Loops, especially, but he would eat Apple Jacks and Sugar Crisp. He would also eat boxes of Lucky Elephant pink candy popcorn. He would have the occasional Pop-Tart. Other than that he would eat scones. I baked scones constantly. He'd have them with cream and strawberry jam. And that was all. So I was worried, a great deal of the time, of course, about his nutrition. But after the

first few weeks, he seemed to get gradually stronger, except for his one wing, which he hid most of the time.

D: So it took a while to adjust to his presence?

I: At first, I was terrified. Not of him, but that he'd come to some harm. Especially when the visitors began coming. I'd never felt so responsible for anything in my entire life.

D: And he never left his coop?

I: Well, at first it seemed that way. He never left during the day or when anyone was around. He crouched down, so that he walked with a stoop. Or he'd sit on the edge of his bed for hours, as though he were in a deep meditation. And sometimes he'd pace and utter things in his angel language. When visitors came to watch him, he usually remained quite still; otherwise they'd be startled. He moved slowly then, deliberately. I felt he was acting then.

D: There was an awareness.

I: He was in pain, and you could tell it was excruciating. I think he was trying to sit through the pain. So the first three to four weeks were all about the presence of this anguish and also coming to terms with the loss of flight. Though I didn't realize this fully until much later. This is how I understand it now though. Of course, I'm not sure.

D: I've been thinking this for a while, but I want to voice it now. That I need to have better questions for this.

I: I had no idea what to ask him. But I felt there was something particular I needed to ask. Even though he might not understand. I had this feeling that if I had the correct question, that in spite of us not speaking the same language, there would be understanding.

D: Obviously, I find the question, the idea of the "question," to be an interesting one. I have often thought the right question is something like a key, but maybe it has more to do with the demeanour, the heart, of the questioner.

I: That in questioning, in probing, in feeling our way forward through this mode of question and answer, there is

meaning in the act itself. Wanting to ask the correct question is a decent stance.

D: But one can't help but notice how much we leave out; how difficult it is to record everything. Smells, sounds, feelings.

I: There was a particular smell that began to emanate from the pheasant coop.

D: Pheasant-like?

[Laughter.]

I: Well, no. And this was the funny thing, I suppose. Because anyone who has kept chickens or other domestic birds, knows the smell of a bird coop. There's a particular mustiness, an acidic scent. So although it gradually built, I suppose, there's a moment when the aroma from the coop sort of hit me.

D: Yes.

I: Well.

D: You seem reluctant to say.

I: Just because it seems so silly, so implausible, and also so terribly clichéd.

D: Okay.

I: It was the scent of ambrosia salad. Do you know what that is?

D: A fruit salad made with pineapple and oranges and coconut and whipped cream?

I: Yes, that citrusy sweet scent. And it was odd, because you almost expected it before you knew what it was, before you could identify it, and maybe before you even breathed it in. Like when you go the fair, you're expecting certain smells, memories of those smells are with you before you actually breathe them in.

I: Did you think to call for help?

D: I was the help. This was made clear to me. I don't know how.

D: What happened to your art-making process during this time?

I: I never stopped taking photographs, though many of them were never developed—just a few. I might still do something with them. I have boxes of negatives. I took photographs of the people standing in line to see the angel. A woman filing her nails. Mothers trying to entertain their babies in their strollers. Toddlers running around. An old man reading the newspaper. Another with a book of poetry under his arm. A woman with a large mirror. I think she planned to hold it up to the angel, but he wanted none of that. There were artists with huge sketchbooks. There were nuns and Buddhists. All sorts of people came in robes. Then it got colder, and colder. The poets still came, the artists. But the ordinary people, if we can call them that, they didn't bother. By the end of November it was very cold and there were many days in a row when no one came. Many women came with their knitting. Oddly shaped pieces—I think some were meant for his wings. Long tubes, for his legs and arms. Toques in colourful combinations with pom-poms. It was all very colourful, and he wore many of the pieces at once. There was the most astonishing cape. He seemed to very much like the cape and used to sit on the edge of the cot with it draped over his back, his wings. It was the most colourful piece of all. Maybe they were influenced by the colours in his wing, the one that was visible most days.

D: You took many photographs of birds.

I: I did. I did because they were so very unusual.

D: All of them?

I: I'm not a bird expert, nor a bird watcher, really. I had experience with the domestic birds, the pheasants, ring-necked and goldens.

D: I remember seeing white chickens, too, in one of the photos. They were so incredibly white. I don't suppose that's so extraordinary.

I: No, not extraordinary. They may have come from neighbours across the road, or down the road. I think some of the birds escaped from lake houses. There were bright yellow canaries, blue budgies. They came soon after he came.

D: In the photos…

I: Yes, there were even more birds. From all over the world. The painted bunting stood out.

D: But what did people make of them?

I: I couldn't sell the photos. People thought they were a hoax. They didn't understand. And I had no explanation. How could they withstand the cold? Without some sort of explanation… they were unwilling to look.

D: Why do you think the birds were there?

I: A message, I think. They were a message.

D: What kind of message?

I: I don't know. Maybe one day it will make sense. Not all messages are clear or make sense, in the way we like things to. Sometimes a message takes a long time to arrive or unravel. To decipher.

D: That's true.

I: There's an image I carry around with me, never photographed. He quite often would go and stand in the yard. Stock-still. In the middle of winter. Once it was snowing, large fluffy flakes spinning slowly down from the heavens. And birds landed on his broad shoulders, he in his white robes and colourful yarn, the magnificent and colourful crocheted shawl covering his wings. And the birds landed on his shoulders, as he held one arm out a little. And he looked up, away, as though waiting for someone, something. Maybe, I remember thinking, he's waiting for a message himself.

D: I can picture that.

I: He stood there for so long. I went and got my camera, but I didn't expect that he'd still be there. He was. His stance was majestic suddenly. He'd gone from a hunched-over, severely injured being in terrible pain, to one that was imposing and regal. This didn't last, but it was as if the

birds—there must have been a dozen of them clinging to his shoulders and arms, and even one in his outstretched hand for a while—had given him a temporary strength. I had an idea then of what he would be like in his full glory. I had my camera, but it didn't seem right to use it. I didn't want the noise of the shutter to scare away the birds. I changed my mind and thought I'd take one photograph. But it was too late. I had waited too long. Just a second too long.

I: It was in December that he disappeared for an entire day. A couple of people had come out to glimpse him that day, and he was gone. I said to them, maybe he won't come back. And they were the last to come out from the city. I really thought that was the end of it, and I was worried, because even though he seemed stronger, he hadn't healed enough. I wandered out late in the day, just in case. I don't know. I hoped I wouldn't find him in a bad way, you know. What would I have done? Something. I don't know what. In any case, I wandered about with my camera. It was cold and getting colder. One of those very bitter winter days. I'd go home and warm up and go back out again. In December it is dark by four o'clock, as you know, and at about that time I saw him coming in.

D: And he was okay?

I: I took some photos. It had begun snowing, that hard uncompromising type of snow. Fine and forceful. I think the photos were quite atmospheric. He hadn't seen me at all, just seemed intent on getting back to his coop. So I let him. I went into the house and made hot chocolate, a thermos full, and took it to him. He accepted it. That's how I found out he'd drink hot chocolate. The coop was very warm—there was a small heater—but the area around him that winter was always warmed, just right. I don't know that he needed the heater. He let me sit with him. I don't know how I knew that that would be alright.

D: And so that was that.

I: Well, no.

D: Yes?

I: Things resumed, that's true. I was alone with the angel, then. Which was a relief.

D: No one cared that he was there anymore?

I: I think it was a matter of other things coming into prominence. There was a hockey player who began performing amazing feats, breaking records. Wayne Gretzky. Maybe people were more interested in him.

D: So it was a relief. But did it also feel strange? Being in this house on the road to the lake, isolated, really, in the middle of winter?

I: I felt responsible in a larger way. I wished at times he would leave. The houseguest that outstays his welcome. But a few days after he'd disappeared for the day, there was a story I heard being told at the general store, which was at the other end of the road, the one by the highway.

D: I stopped in at the store on the way here. It has everything.

I: It's marvellous, isn't it? A real general store.

D: Yes. I bought a pair of cowboy boots and some potato chips.

I: The day that he was missing, a baby was being born on a farm not too far from here as the crow flies. The child was premature, and there wasn't time to drive the mother to the hospital, and anyway no one to drive. An ambulance was on the way, but it was going to be some time. There was just an older child with the mother. The father of the child was away at work. The angel appeared and apparently took care of everything. Everyone is very unclear on the details, the mother especially. And the older girl tells the story, but who listens to a five-year-old? The baby lived, though, and has thrived beyond expectations. The doctors called it a miracle.

D: And were there other miracles that day?

I: There were. There were. An accident on the highway, terrible icy roads. A semi-truck hit black ice and fishtailed. Several cars also lost control and went into the ditch or struck each other, a real pile-up. One woman in the wreckage said that she thought her arm was broken, but it must have been a dream. She'd seen her arm at a strange angle, and she'd felt blood trickling down her face, and then she passed out. When she woke up, she was just fine, but she had this vague memory or dream, she wasn't sure which, of an angel hovering over her.

D: Do you believe in angels? You see, I've been asking myself that question, and I don't know the answer, if you'll forgive me.

I: I know, that's the question. It's a very real question. And maybe it's the only one to ask through all this. But I didn't ask it then. I just accepted things as they were. Alan Watts speaks of the difference between belief and faith… here, let me read this to you:

> We must here make a clear distinction between belief and faith, because, in general practice, belief has come to mean a state of mind which is almost the opposite of faith. Belief, as I use the word here, is the insistence that the truth is what one would "lief" or wish it to be. The believer will open his mind to the truth on the condition that it fits in with his preconceived ideas and wishes. Faith, on the other hand, is an unreserved opening of the mind to the truth, whatever it may turn out to be. Faith has no preconceptions; it is a plunge into the unknown. Belief clings, but faith lets go. In this sense of the word, faith is the essential virtue of science, and likewise of any religion that is not self-deception.

I was inhabiting the unknown, you see. Belief could have no part of it, only faith. However I wished things to be, here

I had to let go. I had no idea what would happen next. It wasn't as though it were written in a book and I could turn to the end.

D: Were there other stories from this day?

I: Oh, at the General Store I'd hear things. On the road from the lake to the store, everyone knew a little about everyone else. Longstanding feuds were healed. Families who hadn't spoken to each other for years were now speaking. A long-lost daughter showed up. People were reunited and there was forgiveness on a large scale. I don't know if it lasted. I hope it has.

[The tape plays for a while and there is white noise, with the occasional ambient sound, voices in the distance, a rattle of what could be china. The ear fills in what might be. At one point I think I hear pages turn. I think I hear the sound of a screen door being opened, slamming. And then there is the sound of wind. There are sounds of weather. It could be the end of the session, or the beginning of another. Maybe the tape was started and stopped and started again, then forgotten. Maybe it's a session that they thought they were recording but didn't. Lost words…]

D: He came into your house one day.

I: There was the day he came into my house. He walked in and walked to this very large coffee table before us. And he lay down upon it, on his stomach, and this is when… this is the first time I really saw his wings. One was bursting with colour, vibrant, and blooming. Each feather seemed alive. Juicy, coursing with colour. This is what the Renaissance and Baroque paintings never really convey. The other one, the broken wing, was drab, and immediately worrisome, though when I looked very closely, not completely without hope. There were places, closer to the feathers' shafts, that held some colour, as though the colour was what kept the feathers alive.

D: He wanted something from you.

I: Yes, but I didn't know what. I reached out and touched one of the healthy feathers and it filled me with a sense of wellbeing. And then, I was afraid, I held my breath and touched one of the lifeless-seeming feathers. It hurt to touch; it really seemed to be speaking its own pain. I didn't want to remove my hand, to stop touching it, though. I needed to know it, this pain.

D: How could you bear it?

I: I couldn't bear it, but I did. It was like that.

[The sound of a whoosh, an outward exhale. Unclear to whom it belonged. And a long pause.]

D: Yes. Can you say more about this experience? It sounds supernatural.

I: At this point everything was supernatural, but it was also very ordinary somehow. That's how life can be, and I had no idea before the angel. He was a mystery, but a tangible mystery. I touched the feathers, the dead feathers. And I felt everywhere he had been, everyone he had touched. I learned that everything affects everyone.

D: What do you mean by that?

I: A flood of experience entered me, and I could feel, see, how one action or occurrence led to another. One person had cancer, and the effects of that changed the courses of everyone around them, maybe just a little. Friends, each member of the family, adjusted things in their everyday lives. But what changed for them mentally made the most difference. Some were more cautious, while others began to live more fully. A few changed directions in profound ways. With others, the changes were more subtle. A sensitivity arose. Or a hardness developed, a single-mindedness. And while all of these course adjustments were shared with me, I also felt the pain of the growth and the sadness and the pain that sometimes accompanies joy, as well.

D: I imagine there was loneliness?

I: I think he was careful at first. Or he tried to be. I think he didn't have the full use of his powers. Which can happen to any of us, when we're down. The loneliness, afterwards. I felt the loneliness was something a person could drown in, touching those feathers. The loneliness from people that he'd walked with, I suppose. Or hovered over, I really don't know.

D: Was he a naturally lonely creature? He seems so apart from everything, from what I've heard so far. I can't imagine being in pain and not being able to communicate; it's what humans fear, really, isn't it? To be in pain, and to be alone and in pain.

I: What constitutes true loneliness? I think we all know the answer to that. The very human answers. I was conscious of trying to not project my own feelings onto the angel. This was difficult, of course.

D: Course adjustments. Let's go back to that. You said he transferred to you all the course adjustments that his wings had made. Something like that.

I: It's hard to explain.

D: It's extraordinary.

I: You don't have to believe it. Or take it on faith. It sounds like a fairy tale. It sounds like a *Star Trek* episode.

D: I can't even take it in.

I: No, I understand.

D: How long did you spend with him on the coffee table, with you administering to his wing?

I: In the end it was three weeks, maybe a month.

D: Really, so long?

I: You see, it was on the third or fourth day. I was cleaning each feather, and they were dense, denser than you can imagine. So many of them. It was like you see on the *National Geographic* specials, when the ducks are caught in an oil spill—a bit like that, but more precise, more time consuming. Each feather needed individual care, you see. But yes, it was on the fourth day, as I became a little less intimidated by

what was before me, I noticed the wire that had lodged and become entangled near the top of the wing, where it joined to his back. I don't think he knew about it, the pain being so generalized and numbing the entire wing, I suppose.

D: It must have been horrible, to see that. You must have felt helpless.

I: Oh, I did, but I also knew I had to overcome that feeling and simply do something. I found wire cutters. Plenty of those around from repairing the pheasant pens. I left him there on the table, and dressed and went out into the cold and rummaged around the old pens that I hadn't been to in ages. I got to work. It took the morning to remove the wire. And while I cut and picked it out, untangled, prying it sometimes, I was overcome by the feelings and thoughts of others. He exuded them, a kind of perspiration.

D: How did you know they weren't his?

I: Oh, I knew. It was impossible not to understand this. They were from elsewhere, filtered through him. A flood. But there were also individual thoughts, discernable. I worked on his wings for a very long time, feather by feather. And so I became more adept at separating the swirl of emotions and events. I could pick out individual stories. Parts of them, anyway. It was all so intimate. The feathers, the stories. I wasn't prepared. It changed me.

D: I suppose it's a silly question, but did you continue to take photographs during this time?

I: No, it's a very good question. It is.

D: Yes.

I: Because. Because that's who I am. What I have always done. Photographing the world is how I understand it. How I see it, make sense of it. And it's also how I center myself, calm myself.

D: I've never seen these photos.

I: I've not developed them. I have the negatives in a box. And I'm not sure if I will. It was enough to take the photos.

And there aren't many. I took a long time composing them in my mind while I was working. And then I'd take a single shot. I didn't want to be intrusive. Besides, I knew exactly what I wanted. There are some photos that when you take them, there's an element of surprise. You end up taking photos you weren't expecting to take. But these were different. Very planned out. Meditative in the process leading up to the shutter being depressed. You see, the wings were enormous. The days were long. Though I would say that even with the shots being planned, I was still surprised by what I saw in the viewfinder.

D: The profound beauty.

I: Yes.

D: Can we slow down here, maybe?

I: Yes, there's too much to say, really.

D: Let's take a breath.

I: I need to stand up and walk around for a bit. Shall we put on our coats and hats and go outdoors for a bit?

D: Yes.

[There are sounds of things being put down. Notebooks, perhaps; glassware, teacups, plates. The sound of someone standing up and the noise of the machine being turned off. The sound of it being turned on again. Settling-in sounds. Someone says, *okay*, off in the distance. A deep intake of breath. Another *okay*. An exhalation.]

D: Shall we just talk about the feathers, the cleaning of them, and call it a day? I'll be back tomorrow. We can talk about the stories then.

I: I think I can manage the feathers.

D: Anything you want to say about them would be fine.

I: Quite honestly, they were magnificent works of art. But, no, more than that. Much more. Each one held its own music, had its own register. The colours, as I touched each one—as they came alive, or tried to, as they awakened—they

were a miracle. I felt as though each feather were a person. Alive in that way.

[Silence.]

D: I can't imagine.

I: I know. I have trouble now, not that this particular memory isn't the clearest thing. Because it is. It's the clearest memory I have. I can close my eyes and I'm there. The trouble is that it's hard to differentiate the memory from a dream. There was something dreamlike about that time, in a hard and difficult way, not airy and light. Dreams can be like that, too. Time moved slowly and quickly as it would in a dream, and it was very heavy, time was. It frightened me a little.

D: Shall we finish there? End here for today?

I: Yes, well, not just yet. First, I want to talk about the way the wire was so entangled in his wings, and that I managed to free him of it. It was the most difficult thing I've done in my life. There were clods of darkness, deep heavy clumps of dirt and debris. His blood, you know, was pure gold. That's how I remember it. I pulled out each bit of barbed wire from his flesh, and then from in amid the feathers on his wing. The golden liquid wasn't copious, but rather quite dear. It was light itself, the material of light. I questioned whether it was actually blood even when I was there, when I was working on the wire, extracting the tangle of it from the honey-like substance and flesh. Because I know that sometimes the eyes see what we want to see. What we expect or hope to see. Sometimes we see even what we dread. I understood why humans invented angels and god sent them to us, in that instant. I understood that religions were meaningless and only god meant something. I understood that everything could fall away and one could simply be in the presence of this love and pain and joy, which is also known as ecstasy.

And how that changes one completely. I understood that whatever is considered to be blasphemous or constraining is wrong. That only love is right. Why wouldn't I have such revelations? The only difficulty is in keeping them with me. Not letting them fade.

I'm a secular person, you should know. And I invented an angel. Yes, I invented an angel.

[A relieved sigh. And another. A silence which seems to be filled with music.]

I: I think we should stop here.

There was a point when everyone hated me, or so it felt. My work had been organized as part of a women-photographers-of-the-prairies exhibit. I had agreed to this. But some of the critics who attended the show were scandalized by my work… they called me a peeping Tom, etc.

D: This was before the angel arrived?

I: Oh yes, sorry, well before. These were the photos of children, the angel children. My photos of innocence. When I took them, I didn't know what to believe, I was just producing the evidence of what I had seen, or thought I had seen, or what had appeared to me. I was innocently photographing innocence. But those viewing the photos saw otherwise. I was shocked. Shaken to the core. It hadn't occurred to me that the photos could be seen as anything other than how I saw them. This was a lesson for me. Up to this point I had been incredibly naïve. It made me realize how unconnected to the world I was.

D: But you didn't change the way you saw the photos? Not everyone saw them in this way?

I: Well, that's always difficult to know, isn't it? The noisy people are the ones we hear, often. Too often. Maybe there were a hundred silent people who found their way to the innocence and wonder I had hoped to convey. The mystery of the photos, which I still see and remember when I look at

them. I worked on them for so long that I can bring up every detail of the images in that show.

D: You kept working.

I: I will never stop working, photographing, looking, seeing. Never. I've always been working.

[A pause. The air, trembling.]

D: I'm glad.

I: It has to be that way. This is perhaps what people don't understand.

D: Yes.

I: I don't mind if it seems I've gone underground, which is one way to see it. Anonymity. I'm quite happy to have intervals where I disappear. But I will emerge. I don't believe in total anonymity. Whatever you make, whatever kind of artist you are, there will be those who want you to go away forever. I don't know why this is. And as an artist there is that feeling you get, that no one wants you, no one cares about your art. None of these things matter.

D: What was it that people were saying, precisely?

I: That I was a voyeur, a peeping Tom. Really disgusting untrue things. They said I was promoting pedophilia. That the photos were sick and unwholesome. Those kinds of things. Nothing could be further from the truth and, of course, these types of statements spoke most loudly of those saying them. My subject was innocence. My subject was faith.

D: They take over your life for a while, these outbursts, this type of criticism. It's horrible.

I: That's exactly what happened. People say you should just grow a thicker skin. But what you need to make art, what needs to happen, is that you must become more transparent, permeable. You have to be able to feel, to let things in. But the world is always at odds with the artist. Maybe it has to be that way. Perhaps I'm sounding imperious here, because I haven't really achieved so much as an artist, not in

the received ways. But I do unashamedly compare myself to great artists. I feel that I'm in their milieu. Not that I achieve their heights, you understand. I'm not so full of myself. But that when I'm trying to situate myself as a human being, as an artist, I jump into that pool.

D: A leap of faith.

I: It's not possible to do otherwise. You'll never be accepted in your own time, not really. And it doesn't matter if you are. At least it doesn't matter that much.

D: Is this true for all artists, do you think?

I: Oh no, some will slip through. But we won't know really which are the ones who will continue to be of interest through time. It certainly won't be me. Does that matter? I don't think so. One is compelled to make art, to record the evidence of our time that is interesting to the artist alone. If anyone else later finds it of interest, then this is not the artist's business.

I: I don't want to forget to talk about halos. And how the artist can adopt a stance that is between the world of this, now, and the mysterious other one that we can't know about. There are no halos in the photographs, and yet they're there. The felt halo. Do you know what I mean?

D: Oh yes, yes, that's exactly what I've been trying to put my finger on.

I: It's the intangible thing, the narrow thread of a life, the *beingness*. Some might say *aura*.

D: I've had a theory swimming around in my head. It's more than a theory. Tell me what you think of this. That we are very close to the other realms. And once in a while, with both a great effort and none at all, we slip into them, just briefly, for a shorter expanse than a blink of the eye. But this is transcendence, this is god, this is heavenliness. This is a hallelujah, pure song, pure delight. And the great artists and writers, they've slipped into this, maybe with a paintbrush or some words. Once you know it's there, it changes you. It changes everything.

I: And then you give that sliver of the other realm back in the art you make. And there are auras that form around that work. There are halos. But everyone has a halo, a kind of aura, if you take the time to see it. Seeing the halo is love. The halo is a kind of jewelry that asks to be stolen. One must go through it, take it, give it, receive it, dive through its center. We think of halos as those depicted in Christian art, but holy people in the art of many cultures have halos: a solid disc, a golden ring, sometimes large ones that surround the entire body, and sometimes taking the form of flames. Near the end, there were moments when all I could see was flames around the angel.

[The energy is palpable, electric. The pause is short but feels long.]

D: The angel got better.

I: Yes, the angel got better. After the wire was removed, after he was disentangled, he got better. It was such a relief.

D: You took photos of the wire tangled in his wings. They were quite close up.

I: And the barbs were so deeply lodged. It was sheer brutal agony getting them out. For him. I don't know how he survived it. It was difficult for me, too, obviously. I'd never witnessed such pain. I hope never to do so again.

D: Excruciating.

I: I pulled out each barb; some were hard to extract. I cleaned each feather. At each stage I took just one photograph. I cleaned the wing with soap and water with broad strokes when I was done. There were thousands of feathers. I would clean them and clean them again. Then dry each one, tenderly and carefully and slowly. As I cleaned, they brightened; life came into them, juice, colour—slowly the colour came back, a surge of colour. It was like when you polish very tarnished silver. You can't imagine it will really shine again. You polish and polish. And then suddenly, the silver shines. The lustre!

D: When did you know that what you were doing was working?

I: I would see him outside early in the morning. I'd be drinking my coffee and looking out the front window of the covered porch. The sun had just come out and it was early spring. The snow had just melted. And he was out there furling and unfurling his wings, together and then one by one.

D: What was that like?

I: Oh, it was magnificent. Magnificent. Pure joy. I took photos one morning. Through the window, the dusty window. And still you can see how glorious it was. Calisthenics for angels. A kind of heavenly Tai Chi.

D: Was it in the spring then, when he left? He did leave?

I: For some reason, people started arriving at the gate again. Parking their cars on the road and just walking up my shale driveway. Uninvited. A few tried to give me some money to see him, and I just shook my head. By then it didn't seem right, I don't know. I could feel that their intent wasn't in the correct spirit. When they came in the fall, so many of them had been curious and hopeful. But these people in the melting snow were desperate and self-righteous and pushy. They seemed to be so sure of themselves. A few of them were bullies, pushing past me when I asked them to leave. They strode to the pheasant coop purposely, and I worried, but I needn't have.

D: Why?

I: Well, by this time, they couldn't touch him; they wouldn't have dared. He was on the rise, anyone could see. His powers were returning. And there was the feeling, I think, there was the feeling... well, let's say they seemed unsure. I was told by one man that the angel knew him, knew what he'd done. It could go either way for him, he thought. He'd wanted to hurt the angel, but now, he was too afraid to. I was shocked, but there were so many

people who had unusual ideas about why the angel was there. Each person took his being there in an intensely personal way.

D: Yes.

I: These are the memories that are difficult to gather. There were so many ideas that I overheard or that were put to me, all so strange to me. It's difficult to remember things that are distinctly at odds with one's own experience and observations. At first it didn't occur to me that anyone would want to hurt the angel, but this was common, a crowd would gather and they would begin talking. What should be done? they would ask. And why, I wondered, were people fine with a very hurt angel, and not one who was vigorous, and gleaming…

D: They were afraid.

I: Yes. And maybe they didn't like questions without answers. The angel himself was a question. His very presence was the question.

D: Just being there, his existence, that would pose a question. But he wasn't answering them. Did he ever speak?

I: He didn't. This didn't mean we didn't communicate. Well, perhaps you could say that it was mainly that he understood me. I didn't understand him, but I learned to be simply open in his presence. To stay with the mystery of him. Not that I didn't want to know more about him, but I saw that my role was to be okay with not-knowing, as it were. I was to attend to him. To attend. At the same time, this felt like learning a new language, no different from learning Italian or Spanish. The language of silence has as many parts of speech as any other language.

D: Isn't this really how it is with human interaction—learning a new vocabulary? We can't really know each other. We're talking to each other and missing this and that. We're withholding parts of ourselves, or trying to present ourselves a certain way. And so the person we're talking to is always a bit of a mystery even when they're trying to be completely transparent.

I: Okay, yes. Yes.

D: So what happened then? What did people do to express their distrust or fear, or whatever it was?

I: Honestly, terrible things. But mostly they threw things at him. One person threw whatever dirt and gravel they could gather as they covered the ground between the front gate and the pheasant coop, his home. And another gave him a paper bag full of apples, apples that were poisoned.

D: And he didn't react.

I: He acted as though he were oblivious. Almost as though he couldn't see them, as though he were behind a two-way mirror. He was in a different dimension. Things were now, especially, altering. The air surrounding him felt different. He was elsewhere, and yet firmly here. He still ate cereal. More and more of it. Pop Tarts. A lot of whipped cream. Trays of scones and jam. I could hardly keep up with the jam, I was always going to the corner store to buy jam. They must have wondered.

D: Did it still feel ordinary? If that's the right word?

I: He started coming in the house. He'd sit down on the arm-chair where you are right now, and he'd open the newspaper I'd have left on the coffee table. He'd open it and flip through. Did he read it? I don't know. I think he must have. His presence was immense. He filled the entire room, not necessarily physically, but I remember the feeling that his wings were expanding. The space he took up was complete. He filled up every particle of the room. When I breathed, I breathed in angel.

D: And the scent was……

I: Ah, the scent…

D: Do you ever wonder how he got here? I mean, it's remote, it's Canada. It's really an obscure spot. One doesn't expect angels to fall out of the sky here. Nothing ordinarily happens, does it?

I: Oh yes, I do wonder how he got here, but almost the entire time he was here, that fall and winter, and then

through the spring, I hardly thought about it. It just was. He was here. I assumed that his appearance here was quite random.

D: Maybe it was.

I: But now I wonder. Perhaps there was more deliberation than I would have then supposed.

D: You think he was coming here, precisely *here*? To see you?

I: Maybe not me, but maybe here, around here. Well, the mystery remains, I don't know really. But just because I don't know or can't understand why, doesn't mean I don't believe that there was a reason for him being here.

D: Did it have to do with your photographs, do you think?

I: No.

D: Does every artist have an angel, maybe? Only you could see yours? Yours appeared to you. Yours was injured and needed your help, and maybe the ordinary angels of artists remain in their own sphere, watching, like in the movie *Wings of Desire*?

I: This is an interesting theory. The best answer I have related to all things about the angel is, *I don't know*. It's the most honest answer. I don't know.

[A pause. It would be a leap, but I want to transcribe this space, this pause, as two people smiling at each other.]

D: What was the general feeling, having an angel about? Was it weird? Uncomfortable?

I: Not so much uncomfortable as overwhelming. All my senses were heightened during his stay, but I also felt, at the very same exact time, incredibly calm and serene. I knew that everything would be okay. But yes. He would pace in the house. And then he would pace outside. Then he would walk off, wings furled. He brooded. He was such a presence. His pain seemed to have subsided, but he was still healing. I would follow him to the top of a low hill, beyond the rows

and rows of empty pheasant pens, and I'd stay behind one of the pens, peeking out. I'm sure he knew I was there. He'd furl and unfurl his wings, attempting, I think, to have them operate in unison. Practicing, relearning, even. Rehearsing.

D: There are photographs of the angel on a large mound, a hill. There are trees in the background. The photographs are taken from below. One can see how vulnerable the angel is at the same time as he is majestic and awe inspiring. And yet, no one thought the images were real? You haven't really shown them at all. I'm looking at them now on the table. You've blown them up to eight by ten inches.

I: I showed them to an art dealer who'd been interested in my work before. Who'd shown work of mine previously. He thought they were childish and manipulative. He assumed I'd hired a model. That I'd played tricks.

D: Emphatically not a trick.

I: It didn't matter. These photos couldn't be shown. Not now. Not for a while.

D: Some time though?

I: I can't imagine the time.

D: If you had been a man…

I: Oh, it might have been different. I might have been taken seriously. What can you expect? This is how it is for women.

D: I should mention here that you're shrugging. [Laughter.] Should we have a little red wine, after that thought? I brought a bottle. I have it here in my bag.

I: Let's.

[The tape is stopped and resumes again, who knows how much later.]

D: We were talking about the angel on the hill, and your photographs.

I: There are the images, and then there was the experience. I watched for some time before depressing the shutter.

So there was a lot going on in between each frame. You see, for me, taking a photograph is about so many things, and in this context, there was a kind of culmination. I was able to put into practice my belief, my feelings, about the art form. I believe, you see, that it's necessary to photograph love; that good dreaming produces good photographs. Everything you are and everywhere you have been go into the photograph. Along with that, all the moments on either side of *the moment that is the photograph* also go into the image that is made. Perhaps this is why I have heard it said that a photograph has the ability to see into the future. At some future point, whoever is looking at it will know time travel. But here, I'm talking too much, when I very much feel that the artist's job is not to speak about their work, but only to make the work. Too much talking ruins things.

D: But sometimes it helps, don't you think?

I: Who does it help? I wonder. Eventually the work is resolutely, incontrovertibly alone, and the artist cannot be consulted. It must speak for itself. It must stand up on its own two feet. If we love the art, we must allow this. Also, we must allow viewers to develop discernment.

D: This can be a problem, can't it?

I: Of course. It is a huge obstacle.

D: What can be done?

I: Nothing, nothing.

D: Really?

I: Those wishing discernment will make some effort to develop their taste, to learn, to be open but to also meet the work, to develop a context for it. To understand composition and form. To cultivate feeling. Yes, feeling. We have the capacity as humans to do all this and more, but seldom seek to do so.

D: A symptom of our location? Perhaps.

I: How do we encounter what we see? As the viewer, what is our responsibility? How does seeing work? Is seeing believing? These are endless questions for me. If we could lose our fear and truly become free in making art, then maybe the rest

of the world could also learn to become free. And by *free*, I mean sharp and innocent and incorruptible and utterly clear. We are scandalized by such humans, and this makes it hard for them to create the necessary space they need.

D: Space, yes. Your work wanted solitude. You wanted solitude.

I: Yes, yes.

D: And yet…

I: There was an enormous presence in my house. Enormous. I never knew when he would come in, enter. When he started coming into this small house, it was a second kind of arrival.

D: You found this frustrating? An irritation?

I: I found it to be a gift. A difficult gift.

D: You cleaned his wings. But that was a more organized effort.

I: He would come in and he would lower himself very slowly to the coffee table. I would gather my sponges and cleaning solutions. Dishwashing soap and water, mainly. And then it would begin. After a couple of hours he would clear his throat, or something, make some sound or small motion. And I knew we were done for the day.

D: What was the cleaning like for him, do you think?

I: The sensations, each tendril, each feather, each part of the feather had feelings, I think. Pure pain at first. But there was an element of release as each feather was restored to lustre.

D: And then he was gone. At some point he left?

I: I was surprised that it was less relief that I felt when he left, but anger. I felt bereft.

[Here there is a pause with a fair amount of crackling. Is it the tape? Or the energy in the room? I can feel a gathering of energy and an indecision. There is some fumbling as if the tape machine is about to be turned off, but then not. Do I hear the words *no* and *okay* being whispered?]

D: You spoke about doubt when we were rummaging in the kitchen earlier for the tea things.

I: I had no doubt concerning the angel.

D: But the photographs.

I: The doubt wasn't about the angel in the photographs. Only the doubt in myself. Concerning my own worthiness. I was certain about the photographs, though. I knew what they were.

D: The artist's uncertainties are not necessarily tied to the work.

I: Exactly.

D: And then he left. And no one came to see him anymore.

I: There were a few stragglers who thought he would come back. The man who had read him poetry when he'd first arrived and couldn't move, he returned. He wanted to talk to me, though he'd not before. No one had. His theory was that maybe the angels have lived here all along and are not from the heavens. They were here before we were and hide, or perhaps it was simply that we cannot normally see them. But I didn't really want to speak with anyone.

D: You mentioned that others wanted to think of him as something from a new-age book. Which you disliked.

I: We have all these ideas of angels. And maybe others have experienced them differently. But he was earthy. Ill mannered, often. Loud at times. Incomprehensible. Mostly he was silent. I've never met someone more silent. There was a radius of silence around him. For me, it wasn't a question of understanding him or what he was, so much.

D: Did he have a name?

I: It wasn't for me to name him, and he offered no name. When he first arrived, I tried to inquire about him, his nature, his name. But he couldn't communicate. And then later, I do feel like he could have, but declined to do so. And I couldn't argue with that.

D: The last photographs. He's on the hill.

I: He's on the hill.

D: And your vantage point?

I: Was from the bottom. He seemed very far away. But when I go to the hill now, when I walk out there, I can see that it's not a very big hill, and the distance is not so very great.

D: He is in full plumage.

I: He is magnificent.

D: He's standing at the top of the hill. And in the next photo his wings are unfurled. I thought to myself, this is the most amazing thing I've ever seen. I want to be closer. As I'm looking, I just want to run up the hill and be near him. Did you feel this?

I: Oh yes. I very much did. I took the photo and walked toward him, up the hill, but just then he took flight. It happened very quickly, I took one shot, then ran to the top of the hill myself. And that's where the other image is taken from. He's directly above me.

[There is the sound of breathing. In and out and out.]

I: I had probably too deeply embedded in my psyche the story of Daedalus, and Icarus, and his makeshift wings, because I fully expected him to come back down. Though, perhaps, that was the scene when he arrived. That was not the scene now. Later I looked up images from the history of art. I tried to find things to remind me. Odilon Redon. The image of Icarus everyone is familiar with, by Brueghel. He was no Icarus.

D: And then there's one last photograph where he's in the sky off in the distance. Then when he was gone, you took a photograph of the sky into which he had disappeared. Is this correct?

I: I did. It was an act of beautiful despair, I suppose. A feeling of utter heartbreak, emptiness, that I needed to

express. But what the photograph doesn't tell you was that… well… And this will test your belief.

D: I'm here.

I: You are. You are.

I: I was in the air; I had risen up. I was suspended. I don't know how far above the ground. I was following him, you see. In my mind's eye.

D: I do. Yes.

I: But this extraordinary thing happened. I don't know how high up I was. I was on the top of the hill, then I was in the air. How to describe this? Well, let me show you something I've never shown anyone.

D: You took a photograph.

I: It was instinct, it was practice, I wasn't even aware that I had taken it. I took a photograph, suspended as I was, in the air.

D: And you printed the photograph.

I: I did. It's here. One minute, I'll go get it. I've hidden it, you see, even from myself.

[Here they are talking to each other from a distance, and their voices are louder.]

D: Why?

I: Because I don't want to remember it through the photograph, but only through the mind's eye, by feeling. But I'll show you.

[Silence. Rustling. The tape is still running. I can hear Daphne whispering. To herself? To the tape. This is unclear. She says: *Irene is looking for the photo in her covered desk. And now she's moving books aside on the shelf. She's pulling out a book. There's a photo emerging from the top of the book.*]

I: Here it is.

D: It's astonishing. My breath is taken away. I'm honestly having trouble breathing.

I: There's that phrase we use, that "seeing is believing." But I don't need to see this photo to remember, to believe. The experience is very much embedded in my soul.

Xaviere
After

What's difficult is wanting to ask questions, to insert myself into the conversation, into the flow and conversation of these two women's voices, which are so apart from me. I know this is impossible. It's over and it's done and I'm left here, alone.

I've reached the end of the cassette tapes. They've had their say. How long have I been sitting at my kitchen table? Days? Months?

What am I to do with my life now?

I've been transformed by what I've listened to, alone, in my apartment, and I don't know what to do about that. My furniture has gathered dust, and the thick *Vogue* magazine on my vintage couch is months out of date. The fashions have all changed since I brought it home with the yogurt and loaf of whole-wheat bread and the large package of M&Ms.

There's another thing. But let me come to that slowly.

I listened and I wrote the words out by hand and I typed them as quickly as I could. I went back and forth over the sentences, and I tried to get each word right, and I think I did. But you still can't hear their voices. I will never get them

out of my head. I hope I never do. I have learned things about listening. About overhearing, eavesdropping. About being quiet. About transcribing. About suspending myself and my thoughts until someone else has the last word.

You see, I have a gift for life. And I wanted to know what I would make of it. I was curious about my life to come, the possible poetry in it. I had bought a bonsai plant strictly for the purpose of letting it grow beyond its confines, placing it on the kitchen table so I could contemplate its progress over my morning poached egg and coffee.

I am 27. I have plans to fall in love, and I can feel it building up in me, this love that I will soon bestow upon a worthy soul. This is what it is to be young, and I am still young. I have plans to fall in love, but what will come of them now?

I knew at the beginning, when I first began transcribing the conversation Daphne had with Irene, that my life was going to change, but I denied it. I worked and concentrated on their words. I concentrated on the tone of their voices. The sincerity, the weight, the way they spoke as if every word meant something deep inside of them.

Now that I have finished transcribing the words of these two women, I feel an urgency. I must do something with the words. I must reveal them, or I must hide them. I don't know what will happen to me now.

I knew there would be this urgency; I felt it even as I slowly and painstakingly captured their words, sometimes in a notebook and sometimes on my typewriter to begin with, before I would type out a good copy. The best copy I am able to make. I have made my copy.

As soon as I heard them talking about children by the lake, their glimmers of wings, their angelic stances, the floating apparitions of wings in air, I began to transform.

Do you remember when you were a child and you imagined powers for yourself? You waited for them to emerge. You were sure. By Grade Three, I wore glasses, for example,

and I was convinced that one day I would have perfect sight, perfect vision. Even better, I would be able to see off far into the distance. I waited for my eyes to improve, and I sometimes walked with my glasses in my hands, dangling from my fingers, hoping that this would be the day my sight was restored, and my vision would be perfect. I would be able to see everything and everybody and into things so deeply and so far off into the distance. I would be able to see right into clouds. Right into the heavens.

I once asked Daphne if she had felt this too, as a child, if she had waited. And she said, "Yes, I'm still waiting. But they will emerge, our powers.

"When I was a child," she said, "when I was a child. I knew that I would learn how to assume other shapes. A tree, of course. But that I could also resume my own shape. That I could take back my human form at will.

"But there was something else," she said. "I already have this power. I can ask people delicate questions and they will tell me their truths. This began when I was a child. And I lost this power, a little; I became too grown up, too self-conscious, maybe. Or afraid, a little. The questions must be advanced in a way that is very gentle. It has less to do with the words, perhaps. You must breathe with the questions; they must float out of you. They must have the best intentions."

Integrity. An innocence.

I only know that I must write this as it happens, feeling my way in the darkness with words.

I thought I understood about transformation, what change was. I often recited Rilke's "Torso of an Archaic Apollo": "You must change your life." I recited it in various tones, but finally settled upon a dry utterance, one that was flat and unequivocal. *Thy will be done.*

I saw myself, I saw my child self, my actual child self and not just the idea of who I was as a child, in the photographs. I remembered the photographer standing amid the trees. We knew she was there. I was there. It was me. I was

one of the children in the forest by the lake. Which one? It doesn't matter.

I knew this, and then I forgot it.

Why would we be made angels and then forget it?

Or were we born becoming angels? I don't know.

I didn't know anything about God, and I still don't. People think that angels are connected to God, but I'm not so sure.

And if angels aren't connected to God, then to what, to whom, for what?

This morning I moved to Irene's house. I packed up a small suitcase and my toothbrush and I took all the food I had in my cupboard in a cardboard box. I stopped at the store by the highway to buy milk and eggs and whipped cream, on the road to the lake, the road to Irene's house.

When I arrived at Irene's, I walked into the covered porch; it was open. And the key to the door was under the welcome mat. I went in and straight to the kitchen. I felt I'd been there before. I put down my supplies and glanced around. I walked out to the living room where the interviews had taken place. Immediately I felt happy and less afraid. Quietly content. My heart stopped racing.

The coffee table.

I thought of lying down on it. Not yet.

There is the painting on the wall, the one of the pheasants. There is the floral couch and the chair Daphne had often sat on while they spoke to one another. She wrote this in her notes. And now I'm sitting in the kitchen at Irene's kitchen table for two, and if I lean forward, I can see where they were sitting in the other room. I might have been here all along.

I don't know where I am in time.

I'm not confused. I just don't know. I'm clear.

I've been called.

I wake up and I'm in Irene's bed, and it really has begun now. Are you wondering if it hurts?

It hurts.

Did you know I had dreams to move to New York? I wanted to be a snob when I came home and say I was living in New York City instead of this dump of a city and maybe really, I'd never return here to Edmonton. Returning didn't really matter. Nothing will matter in the same way again, will it?

Will I write poetry now? Why shouldn't I?

When you look at that sculpture of the goddess Daphne turning into a tree, think of me now. There are branches emerging from my back. It's like that. And leaves, so many leaves unfurling, slow and sticky. The energy this is taking is immense.

This is the most difficult thing I've ever experienced. What a blessed life I've had to this point. I know now that I have to measure up.

I don't want to even write down what I'm feeling because I don't want anyone to have to imagine what I'm going through. It's awful awful awful. I'm in awe. I can't stop any of it, any of it.

Who will watch over me? Who will be my angel? I've never been so alone. I'm crying out. I came here to Irene's house to cry out. You see, I needed to be alone for this.

What is this? A metamorphosis? But more painful than Kafka's Gregor turning into an insect. He just woke up that way. I'm fully conscious of every change, every feather erupting—the heaviness, the new weight I'm expected to carry. I have to balance myself differently; I need to learn to walk again. My bones are becoming lighter and my back is an open wound. It's just beginning.

Mama!

I think days have passed. I have a vague recollection of the sun going down, of intervals of darkness and intervals of light.

It's another realm. I begin to know things. I feel compassion for all beings in a radius that is larger than I can now

comprehend. My awareness of being in this realm started small. The radius of my compassion began with those people who live on this road to the lake and expanded all around the lake. It goes on increasing in size. I'm dizzy sometimes. But my breath grows stronger; my lungs are larger. My lungs are new and efficient. I can't believe how powerful they are. It's like having once been an old sedan, and now I'm a Ferrari. I'm a Lamborghini.

Time is passing strangely. I think this is because I'm thinking thoughts without really thinking them. I've gone behind thought; I'm through it. At times I'm immersed in such beauty that I forget about the pain. The sensation is not like being drugged, though, because I still feel everything, every single change at the cellular level, each exquisite cell. We forget that our bodies are such works of art.

Sometimes I spend a day with one word, feeling each letter of it with my tongue, and then going deep into the meaning of it and seeing where it has travelled and how the word has been used through time. Yesterday, it was the word *delicate*, and today I'm going to deep-sea dive with the word *silence*. I'm going to float in the clouds with it.

The choice of these words is not accidental. The arrival of words rarely is. I didn't choose them; they merely appeared to me. My body is becoming delicate like a bird's. I have to hold myself carefully now, as I would cradle a bird. Even though I am becoming powerful, I'm also delicate. When I hold a small bird in the palm of my hand, I'm careful; I'm aware of the living, breathing thing that might be holy, but might also use its beak to stab my palm. I don't want any retaliation. I couldn't stand that sort of pain, the sort that comes from fear. So I attempt to hide any trembling, I hold my soul perfectly still, I breathe as though my life depends on it, and the oxygen is very pure now. The bird is warm and downy, and when you hold it for too long it begins to feel a bit damp, and the air around it musky.

Yesterday was the word *delicate* but today the word is *silence*. The kind of silence that you can create yourself, even

though you don't have any control over who you will become or what you will create. Silence is a luxury like sweet cake is a luxury. For weeks now or days—I can't decide how to count time any more—I have lived in utter silence: the silence of emerging, the silence of lake cottages in the off-season. What I am living is the silence of a forgotten artist late in life, and I can imagine my creations with a bright, fierce, terrible clarity, and there is no one to stop me. No one. I am that alone.

I once went to a concert that was so loud, I became blind to the music and the world around me. Everyone and everything were vibrating. You'd think that only your hearing would be affected, but I started to have blurry vision and was dizzy and off-kilter. I felt drunk. I left partway through because I couldn't stand this way of being. I left the concert stadium and jumped into the first taxi I could catch. I put my hands over my ears and asked the taxi driver to turn off his radio. The inside of the car was so quiet. We were moving but I couldn't hear a thing. It was dark and there was a swishing of lights, the trees in the boulevards going by out the window, the tall buildings. When I emerged from the taxi, I kept my new silence with me.

I'm moving so fast, and yet for hours I'm perfectly still. I'm using every ounce of energy to create the colours of these feathers, the harmony of the colours together, and their vibrancy when isolated from the rest. Innately I know that the design of my wings will dictate how I fly, the ways in which I will rise. There is meaning in each eruption, each brushstroke. Am I making them, or are they making me? I don't know, but I lose myself in them.

I've lost myself. I've lost myself to this new self who is also me and also everything I have been; I retrace the steps of everywhere I have been and fold these into the new being, me. Even though I think I know her, there are times when I see her off in the distance, in a landscape, as though in a photograph. Maybe the photographs are Irene's; I don't

know, but I think they are, even though I saw so little of her work. I know her work from the words I transcribed. Try this: write down the words of someone else with a fountain pen and you'll see what I mean. Ink is more than you think it is; it's a kind of air that you breathe together in a small enclosed space.

I'm lying on top of the white bedspread on Irene's bed, and even though it's been days, it's still pristine, and I don't know how I've managed this. I sometimes lie on the angel's coffee table and I pretend it's a massage table. There is a colourful crocheted blanket at the end of the bed, and I clutch it to my chest, and later I fold it carefully and place it there again. I don't want to disturb anything. I need some feeling of order in my life, and the crocheted blanket gives me stability.

Am I afraid? That might be the same as asking me if I'm happy. But in fact I am both of these things. If happiness can be said to resemble joy, if happiness can be said to encompass agony. The pain has become a constant—excruciating but reliable. Until you can do this for days, the miracle of being able to not think and only feel is too academic. To feel without thinking about the feelings, the sensations, but to merely allow them to stand… what a rarity. Although maybe it will be like this for me now. All nerve endings and sensations.

The answer, though, thank you Sylvia Plath: I am, I am, I am.

I'm making progress. I open a window. I'm able to stand for longer intervals without feeling intense vertigo. I stand at the window in Irene's bedroom. I've smoothed out the bedding, I've tidied things. I've folded the white and colourful crocheted blanket. I study the white borders of it, the pretty pink, lime green, turquoise. I think I might like to read something. I'm craving something like a *People* magazine or *Vogue*. And then the birds start arriving.

The birds. I don't know why I'm surprised by the birds. I knew it could happen. I had listened to Irene describing the

birds arriving. As a child, *Cinderella* was my favourite Disney movie because of the way the birds helped with the ribbons.

They came last night when the pain was severe and stayed until the sun rose. I had left the window open, or the window had been open. They arrived, they entered, and they spoke to me, sang, they were a comfort. One sat on my shoulder. They gently picked at the feathers attempting to protrude, erupting from my new wings; they pulled them and preened; they knew what to do. They taught me things and I absorbed. They were shy but careful and understanding. Birds are not what I thought they were.

They're gone now. They left when the sun was rising. I think they'll come back. I'm not yet finished.

I have a friend, Avery, who has to listen to music all the time. She wakes up and turns on the radio, and then she plays music every chance she can get. She listens to the car radio, and at work, she has a radio on her desk. At home after work, she puts on record after record. The Rolling Stones, The Smiths, Talking Heads, Blondie. Sometimes she dances and sways and sings, and at other times, she barely attends to what is playing. She'd be worried that I've spent so much time without music, but the thing is, I haven't. Maybe it's silence, but the music in silence is a symphony. It's astonishing and holds me and lifts me up. One minute the cellos are coming in, and the next the flute, the piccolo. Sometimes there are solos that are heart-stopping.

This entire morning I've spent thinking about heavenliness and how it is really a form of earthliness. Thomas Merton believed that all things had a heavenly existence, which he said was "an indescribable spirituality and lightness." The "true nature of the earth" is heavenliness. Heavenliness as a "gift of love and of freedom." But he also realized that it is "born partly of physical anguish." He was right, and I am living it so that others can have their heavenliness without the anguish. Or is there no heavenliness without anguish? I don't

purport to have all the answers. I only lean toward hope, trying to keep my balance, as this fiery diadem arrives on my head. This very heavy world that I now balance on my crown restructures the world before me, a miracle that is performed for me alone. I have to be careful when I look left or right, or it could all collapse. The world ablaze. A hinted smile and a queen's wave. I'm practicing, but there's no room for error.

Now I'm learning to breathe all over again. For days my breathing has been ragged, uneven, and I worried that I would not be able to make this transformation being asked of me. Given me. I had the terrible urge to cry out—my spiritual longings, my grief, and my fear of what I'm giving up—but my breathing didn't allow it. I have a feeling that I am truly being reborn, and as I adjust to this new breathing, I align to the dimension I'm now in.

My lungs are different. The cells are jewels, nearly invisible, so light. They take in light and air. If they could be examined and reproduced, I think anyone could fly. These new lungs have so many gleaming facets that if you could strike a match and hold it up to them, the colours and twinkling light would make you give up all your ideas of disco balls, of stars and the blazing universe.

My fingers are also new. Writing this is a new sensation. My fingers are so light now, you see. Sometimes I write in my notebook merely for the sensation. It reminds me of who I am, even as I'm changing. My cursive has more flourishes now; I don't know how that has happened, but my handwriting is what I always wished it had been. Before it was choppy, part cursive and part printing. And now it's lovely and so elegant, like you would have been taught before the typewriter was invented. But it has its own personality, too. You would know it anywhere. Beautiful and flowing and light. So uniform. Even so, it's still my hand moving over the soft white paper, the pen hugging the faint blue lines, making exquisite flourishes that even I have to stop and admire.

I'm writing for the sensation, but I'm also writing to hold myself together, to save my life, to save it, and maybe even cherish it a little. I'm writing my way into the next realm.

I realize that it's always been this way, but when I write, I come closer to understanding what it is to exist.

The sun woke me up this morning with its wild blinking. I realized that it would make sense to pray to God, but I don't know who God is, and I don't even know what to ask for. Are these wings the sign of someone or some god blessing me?

I've never thought I'm anyone special. I'm not. I'm the most ordinary young woman in the world. I still can't believe that I've been chosen. The only possibility is that this is random. I'm an accident. I've become abstract, like a painting. And I'm a story that is utterly unbelievable and yet you can't stop turning pages.

I exist because Daphne existed. I exist because she asked questions and recorded them on cassette tapes. I exist because I wrote them down, because I copied her words and they entered my bloodstream.

Now I've entered an even deeper state of solitude. I don't need to explain myself to myself. I don't need to know why. Even so, I find questions arriving. I don't try to answer them, but do as Rilke advised: I try to love the questions. Why didn't I know the power of solitude before now?

When you're giving birth to yourself, it's evident that you can do anything, be anything. The fullness of your powers in relation to the universe is present, and I know I have to do everything I can to stay with it. This feeling could disappear very quickly if I let it, but I hold it to my heart tenaciously; I guard it as fiercely as a wolf would protect her young.

Creating this huge space around me so that my wings could exist, even if I didn't quite know what they were or why, I didn't have to ask if there was god. God was. But God was the air and the air was God. I was breathing, you see. And my lungs were becoming jewels, light and iridescent

cells, royal blue, purple, ruby red, juicy and glistening. As I breathe, I can taste them, these colours. They're marvellous and filling and very good for me, like candy but packed full of nutrients.

I know I'm not special. Every life contains those moments when you're in the presence of a greater power, something greater. I've felt them already, I've heard them, far off. They're happening right now. But people step away from them so quickly, afraid or in denial. They resist them so that they can continue exactly as they have been.

Only now does it occur to me to take a photograph of myself. I should have taken one when the wings were emerging, their damp birth, like trees erupting from the earth, torn, after a storm, their roots huge and surprising and wild. The violence of it might surprise even me.

I open a closet and find shelves of cameras. Irene's cameras. But there is one, the one I know she took photographs of the angels with, and I set that one up on a tripod. I find a roll of film in a box that is unlike the other boxes, covered in dust.

I set the timer. This feels human, this act of allowing for the passing of time with a gentle ticking. I hardly need the interval, though, as I can move before the camera, move into that light space before the lens by blinking my eyes. I think that's how I do it. The film advances and I advance with it.

I move my wings, up and down; I'm vigorous, I'm poetic. I'm majestic. I take 36 photographs, but it's the last one with which I'm most pleased. Then I rewind the film and put it into a black canister. I leave it on the shelf in the closet. The light of me will arrive at some point in the future that I cannot presently determine. But it will arrive.

The last photo? I was floating. I was thinking about something so beautiful that I had entered the silence of flowers. I could feel myself lifting, rising up. I was so light. The colours in my wings reached an apex, the colours themselves

throbbed, and new colours were born. My feet hung down; my eyes closed. You can imagine the rest.

At this point I realize how unbelievable this is. I am living the unbelievable. I haven't made a noise for days, but now I laugh out loud, just quietly. At myself. No one could believe this. I couldn't, and yet I could. There's nothing like pain to make something plausible. I know at this point that whatever happens next, this is my reality, and I refuse to keep it to myself. It must be uttered. I must not hide from it. My life will be an utterance: the possibility of flight.

Reality is full of secrets that everyone knows and refuses to acknowledge.

I'm writing something so implausible that no editor would dare touch a word because it makes no sense.

I pledge to write only what dazzles me and what fills me with love for the mystery of who I am becoming, with complete disregard for a desire that anyone believe in me.

Even though I feel the importance of writing every nuance of every sensation of this emergence, I know that I'm missing things.

Such as: sometimes I hear music that is being played by a faraway orchestra. Or I hear a young woman learning the cello, playing in a light-filled room before she's had her breakfast. I can hear her stomach rumble as she leans into the notes and the light coming in from the Venetian blinds warms her bare feet.

Further off a child is stirring her bowl of cereal, quickly, so that it splashes over the edge of the bowl. A small act of rebellion.

A woman is in bed with a book, and I can hear the pages turning, and the way she's sighing at what she's reading. What is the book? The book is *Middlemarch* by George Eliot, and she's at the part where Dorothea renounces her fortune.

A man is riding a bike; it's early in the morning, a country road. He's about to hit a loose patch of gravel. He's about to lose control.

The wings have wholly emerged; I am in full plumage. Can I say that I'm in awe? Of myself? They are part of me, but they are their own entity. They are me, but they are also *with* me. I'm tired, I'm euphoric. I want to try them out, yet I know it's not quite time for that. They're strong, but I need to be equally strong.

I need to know things that I will only learn by knowing them. I need to know the sky, and so I walk out of the house and spend a day sprawled out on my back on a grassy hill, *his* grassy hill. For days after the wings were "finished" I was tender with them, as you would be with a newborn, but then I discovered that they're sturdy and more malleable than paintings of renaissance angels would suggest. They were lovely to rest against, pillowy and comforting. They held me and I felt loved.

I want to dwell on this thought. I had been craving love so badly. I was longing. I needed small caresses. I think of how someone looks at you a certain way when they love you. They push your hair out of your eyes, off your cheek. They touch you because they can't not touch you. They run a finger along your cheek or on the inside of your wrist or trace the indentation at the base of your neck, along your collar bone. They are entirely unaware of how this affects you, but they cherish you so wholeheartedly the sweetness of it is profound, and you know you will take that to the grave; you will live it as you fall into death. It affects everything throughout the entire length of your puny glorious existence. And now for me, that longing for love, which would have been sent outwards, is now satisfied and housed in the soul, becoming exquisite and wildly centering.

I stare at the clouds and the delicious blue sky, and they're new in the way that aliens landing on earth would be new. My eyesight has changed. Colours are clearer, deeper; they have a taste. I can see great distances, and then up close, blades of grass are miracles, worlds. The dew on a leaf mesmerizes

me for an hour. Everything is magnified. I say to myself, out loud, over and over: *to see is a miracle*.

I lie on the hill all throughout the day and into the night, watching the sky from one morning until the next, never moving, mesmerised. The gradations of colour as the sun rises, and then the clarity of the blue that swallows me whole. I cut into the sky as an Olympic diver would expertly tip from the high board at an outdoor pool in the summer. It's inevitable. Soon I will be in the water of the sky, and I won't even feel the cold when I arrive.

A hawk flies over, and there is a beautiful and sharp disturbance in the frequency of things. High up a seagull spots me, and we look into each other's eyes. I'm changed again. A murmuration of sparrows arrives and dances above me, and the music that they make with the air is so profound and delightful. I'm laughing and crying, and they send me messages on the rising and falling notes about how to live in a state of grace. I fill and I empty and I close my eyes and open them and I am free. I understand what being free is and how to clear a path for myself.

In the golden hour I lose myself. The word *heaven* comes then. Of course it does. And this is where I discover my power to daydream my way right into a scene. I feel myself flying among and amid the golden and glittering drops of light. I can hang and hover, held up by the honeyed air. It's so playful, the light at this hour, it's not the least bit serious, unless you consider the music of Mozart to be serious. The golden hour was invented to illustrate joy, an effervescence. I'm floating inside a glass of champagne; its bubbles make me laugh and feel loose and utterly splendid.

And when I'm finished with the sky (though I know I'll never be finished with the sky) I'm called to pay attention to the grass and the trees. I understand leaves now in a way I never have before. Trees are angels. Their bark can be read like braille, and I walk through the trees and feel each one, closing my eyes. The birch trees are soft and silky and peel and curl with black dark moments, and their spirit is kind

and steely. Black poplars are dark and furrowed and are natural storytellers, and they know more than is possible for their age. White poplars were designed to tremble, and their leaves dance at the slightest breeze, and their bark is both smooth and old at the same time. They are wise and pleasant.

I never want to leave the trees: they've told me so much, wise teachers. They understand me, too. Each spring they recreate themselves, summon up all the juice of life and burst forth, green and lovely. But you must know how difficult it is for them, to be so exuberant when the earth is in such pain. Humans inflict so much upon them. Still, the trees fulfill their destinies, and with panache. New branches erupt slowly, fledglings. And then one leaf, and another, hundreds and hundreds, until the tree is flying in the wind.

What is being asked of me? I must consider that the answer to this desperate question is that nothing is being asked of me. What decisions should I be making? I'm merely existing. Becoming. But no, it's more than that. Why had I never asked myself before, *how do you want to be*? It's not a matter of being prepared, or not being prepared.

Having wings or not having wings can't possibly be what makes a person an angel, can it? Am I being asked to invent my own spirituality?

I thought I was through the agony of birthing these wings, but I'm not. All last night I howled and yipped and yodeled with the coyotes as if the real purpose of this pain were to join me with the universal cry. I howled more like a wolf, but the coyotes still accepted me. This acceptance nearly destroys me and makes me whole. This morning I feel like I'm connected to all the creatures who live in my surroundings. I didn't know there was so many. Chipmunks and squirrels and mice. A mile away from here is a fox, and there's even a family of badgers… A stream flows from the lake, and there are beavers. There are fish with them, frogs. A beautiful stag is walking through the forest right now and six does, picking their way so easily and carefully. A moose

is further off, and he's majestic and vulnerable and bold and just a little bit haughty.

Am I to look after the world?

Does this mean I can never become a mother? Right now I'm feeling limitless, but I also know that things have been torn away from me—human things, small homely things—moments, gestures, simplicity. The scent of a newborn infant in my arms. The feeling of a small child's arms tightly around me. The unconditional love of my own child. I'll never experience the wild joy my own child would express, being pushed higher and higher on a swing, looking back at me with love and glee.

Will I drink a glass of water in the same way? Will everything hold a different meaning? When I pick up the glass and raise it to my lips, what will it signify?

Will I write my poetry? How will I experience those ordinary things that I want to write about? What is writing when you are obligated to look after the world? Could they even be the same thing?

And what about happiness? Just the everyday happiness of reading a book on a lawn chair on a sunny day? Or of meeting friends at a pub and laughing at the stories they tell over a pint? What about the happiness of walking in the morning on a forest path? Or of being held by someone who loves you? Of someone stroking your hair, or holding your hand? Am I not to have these moments because of what I've become? Am I not to be significant in the lives of friends and family… am I not to be loved?

And yet I can't feel this as a burden. There must be some joy in this, too, not merely obligation. I grow into the joy of these wings incrementally, with some trepidation, but excitement as well. I admit that it feels a bit like Christmas Eve when you still believe in Santa Claus and the magic of gifts arriving.

Today I'm hungry. When was the last time I ate? I know that I still need food, but I also know that I'm not the same; I

need less, and I don't need to eat as often. I remember Irene's angel and how he liked whipped cream and scones and jam. He liked cereal. My new hollowed-out bones require a different array of nutrients.

I haven't left Irene's farm for weeks, but my car is parked outside. I squint at it. It suddenly seems so small. I'm reminded of my new form. I take up space differently. The store is three miles up the road by the highway. I make my wings as small as I'm able and I wear one of Irene's huge house dresses. I drape my neck with colourful scarves, and I wrap one around my waist. I look absurd, but I tell myself it's a bohemian look, which I've seen in a *Vogue* magazine, even if it is an old magazine. I put on round sunglasses and I get in the car.

I drive down the road, at first slowly and then very quickly. I can't help it; I'm driving fast because I want to be flying. It's early and no one is on the road. I can see the air travel by me as you would see the blur of a photograph that focused on the car alone. I see every flower in the ditch, the long grasses swaying gently, the trees looking at me, feeling me, as I go past, and I absorb their energy. Birds follow the car, and I know they're flying with me, too. A butterfly alights on the driver's-side window and clings. I arrive in the gravel parking lot outside the old general store in a small cloud of dust. When I open the door and get out, I put out my finger and the butterfly alights. Its wings are orange and blue and a little bit frayed, but it's a fierce little thing.

I raise my finger to the sky and we stare at each other and the butterfly tells me things. I look at and marvel at all her colours and notice how striking she looks against the blue of the sky. Yes, we say to each other, yes.

I raise my arm just slightly and she flies away. It's surprising how quickly a butterfly can move through the air. I follow her with my eyes until she merges with the sky. The blink of an eye.

Is there a reason for the creature to have appeared? Need I write it down? It seems significant, though I can't easily make

a metaphor of it beyond the obvious one of transformation. I'm wary of the obvious. Sometimes it's enough for a creature to appear and disappear. To make contact and be released.

As I walk toward the store, I pass a man who doesn't acknowledge me. For the first time, it occurs to me that I might be dead. Is he absorbed in his own thoughts? We pass each other and I try to smile, to make eye contact. I wonder how I'll be seen. I'm ignored.

Maybe I'm not dead but exist in some other realm. But no. If I exist in another realm, I also exist in this one, too.

I walk into the old general store; it's a relic from another time. I pick up a basket. They have real baskets and not plastic ones, and it's refreshing. I feel the weight of the basket in my hand and I think, *I must be alive.* Maybe I've just become invisible, but then, no, I walk down an aisle and there's a small child running from her mother, and she looks up at me and grins and turns around and runs back down the aisle.

I had never once thought that this emergence was about anything but becoming more alive. Why haven't I considered it as a death? I would have refused it, though it must say something that the opposite position never entered my thoughts.

I look at all the food, the rows of cereal and the cans of beans, the cooler filled with milk and cream. I wait to see what calls to me. My basket eventually fills.

I take my basket to the cash register, and an older woman is waiting. She smiles at me as though she were waiting for me. I can feel her deep kindness and I wonder if she knows, if she understands. Maybe she, too, has become something with wings. I hesitate to use the word *angel* because no one has told me that's what I am. Is this even necessary? But I realize, at the moment when my oranges and apples and dark purple plums are being rung into the cash register, that I've been waiting, too. For some kind of visitation, an annunciation. A message.

She's wearing a linen apron, one she's likely made herself, and it's lovely, really, the faded blue-grey of it. Her cheeks

are a natural pink, as though she's been outside recently. She puts all my purchases in a box. The cereal and the six loaves of cinnamon bread. The butter tarts and the tea. I've cleared them out of four kinds of chocolate bars. I hand her the money when she says the amount. When we're done and I'm picking up the box, already turning to leave, she says, "Yes, soft and kind." I look over my shoulder and she's smiling, but now I'm wondering if I'm hearing things. I just smile back and nod and go to the car.

Back at Irene's, I unbind my wings, place three Hershey's chocolate bars in my pocket, and walk out. I have that feeling trees must have in the bright spring in a soft breeze. My leaves are new and pristine, just-birthed. The green juice of life is new and vibrant. But the tree is older than the leaves; the offices of the tree are many.

While I've been transforming, things have been happening in the outside world.

I don't need the newspaper any more to tell me what's happening in the city, or in the world. I feel it, I know it. Maybe I don't know everything, but stories filter into my consciousness. I shouldn't be capable of taking it all in, but somehow, I am.

Floods and fires, people fleeing from natural disasters, carrying photos of people they love. But I also know when someone has lost their job, or when a woman's child is stillborn. Great disappointments and personal tragedies. Small things and large things. Just now a woman has dropped a water glass on the tile floor and she has stepped on a large shard. She doesn't cry out because she doesn't want to frighten her baby. A man is thinking about ending his life after losing his job because of a small error. A woman has written her best friend a flaming email, and the friend is opening that email right now.

All I can do is breathe out my compassion and surround them, the idea of them, with my wings. I close my eyes and do this, and it takes every ounce of strength I have at first,

though every day this becomes easier, but also more difficult *because* it's easier. This is so common, I do it a hundred times a day, a new and developing reflex. And I don't know what it means, or if it helps. I know it doesn't change much, but it does change a molecule or two in the entire endless expanse of the universe. It changes the frequency. It changes me.

This reflex doesn't make me holy or religious; quite the opposite, it pares me down to a strong essence and gives me direction, filling me with calm such as I've never experienced. The only thing I can think to name it is love. It's the most difficult kind of love you can imagine.

Something that is new: I no longer feel anxious or self-conscious or bad about myself in any way. I feel confident and beautiful, but not in the undermining ways that beauty magazines encourage a woman to feel. I don't feel the need for thicker lashes or plumper lips. This is perhaps more radical than having wings. I've always been fairly confident, but I know now that I'll never have those fleeting thoughts that women have: I won't feel inadequate, I won't wish I'd said this rather than that, I won't worry about anyone thinking badly of me. I won't worry if I'm misunderstood or if someone dislikes me for no reason.

I walk out into the darkness of morning, just before the sun is summoning its strength to rise and belt out the song of sunrise. The colours are going to be magnificent this morning. I can already taste the delightful popsicle juice of them, the purples and oranges. The streaks of pink are particularly invigorating. I walk to the hill.

I've been waiting, I think, because I thought someone would arrive to explain things to me, to show me how. How to be what I now am.

I now think that solitude, this feeling of being set apart, alone, is part of what I'm to learn. It's intense. I've been plunging into loneliness again and again, as one jumps into shallow water when learning to swim. But now there's no getting out of the water. I am the water.

Who shows a toddler how to walk? No one explains it to them; one day when they're ready, they walk. No one says, firs*t you stand, and then this foot, and then that.* No one explains momentum, balance. All the muscles that expand and contract with each movement.

I've never been in a church in my life except for Daphne's funeral. When members of my family die, they ask to be cremated and secretly scattered in city parks or by the river. So I don't know any doctrine, and I've never studied the bible. My only knowledge of anything to do with angels comes from an introduction to art history course at university or from rolling my eyes at images of new-age angels in greeting-card stores or hung from rearview mirrors. In other words, it's scant, and imaginative, and skeptical.

In art, angels are rarely flying. Maybe some hover. They're annunciatory, always delivering messages, or decorating a scene when the difficult stuff goes down.

Angels aren't birds. They use their wings, but they also use instinct, spirit, soul. I ask the universe for a state of grace and I'm given it.

I wait for the sun to rise. I know it will be easier this way. I don't know what to do, but I try.

I try to imitate flying. I'm alone. The birds are waiting somewhere; they know, too, the necessity of being alone. Entering the air, alone. Only I can lift myself up. And yet it's the beating of thousands of wings that carries me upward and helps me navigate. One is alone and not alone. Flying is that sort of contradiction.

It's with the concentration of an artist in solitude with her painting or a spider spinning her web that I enter the air, creating myself. I fling myself into it quite fiercely, and then I intuit that it must be gentle, and slow, and determined. It must be without thought. I travel a long way, into the sunrise, and am born again and again. I leave the earth, and it's beautiful.

It's beautiful. Beautiful, beautiful, beautiful. Even the word is different now. The exhalation, the tip of the tongue, the fullness.

In the mysterious beforehand, I'd imagined it would hurt, but this is pure music, much closer to dream than to anything. I thought I would be clumsy, that it would require a degree of athleticism, but it was spirit that I called upon, spirit that held me aloft. I had imagined I would need a type of sophistication and a complicated theoretical knowledge, but what was required, instead, was an innocence. The ability to travel into dreams.

I stay in the air most of the day. I travel. I travel into dreams, but I also travel into reality. I have absorbed so many stories and feelings that I'm aching like I would after eating a turkey dinner. But I don't feel ill: I'm in awe. How do people carry around such burdens?

What's difficult is returning to earth and knowing that it must be time. Time for what? I only know that I must reintegrate with society. Which sounds cold and scientific. I'm also afraid, or let's call it a small case of the nerves. I'm not afraid for myself, but for those I know and interact with. How will this affect them?

Even though I have not spoken a word out loud for weeks, I need a day of quiet after my day in the sky and in the clouds. There is a way to be even quieter than quiet, I find. I spend a day going into the quiet within quiet. I find this coming into my power just as moving as embracing the sky and feeling my wings.

It's five in the morning on the day I plan on driving back to my apartment, back to where I once lived and who I was. Am I still?

I look in the mirror and I see questions. I'm not afraid of questions. I know that I'll live them. I'm beginning to understand—mind you, it's a frail understanding—that the questions will now be my raison d'être. I'm beginning to understand that I'll be birthed again and again, bathed in these questions that take me all the way back to the womb. Every new place I go, it will be the same; every new person I meet, the same.

One must reinvent oneself thousands of times. Every morning when I wake up, it will be as if I'm opening into the mystery again. I'll put on my silence, that long translucent robe that will come with me everywhere, always.

I spend an hour looking into the mirror, trying to see just the mirror and not my face. That's how it will be now, I say to the mirror. I will never quite see myself again. I am the secret that is in me, that *is* me. I'll never be done paring myself down to some light-filled truth. I look at the mirror and for the first time I see the mirror, its silvery surface; I see into its depths. It feels like falling asleep after a night of insomnia. You don't know you're falling at last into slumber, but eventually you wake up.

I put my case in the trunk of the car, and I look up at the sky, and it calls me again, so I go briefly to it. I don't know when I'll be this free again, even though I know I'm always free, now I'm free. The sky is a brilliant blue, and I'm vain, I want to feel the juice and colours of my wings against it. I have a greater understanding of those artists who are virtuosic because I've learned how difficult it is to create true beauty. The kind that is experienced by the painter who has an unearthly command of their paintbrush and doesn't even have to think about the colours or the brushstrokes. Their hand moves over the canvas in a holy state of inspiration and skill, and it's as simple as taking a breath. They take over the world that way and meet God in a magnificent euphoria. The hand breathes in and out, and later, if you're invited to hold that same hand, you're holding the hand of someone miraculous, someone who understands God.

I come back down to earth, and I fold myself and my wings into the small driver's seat. I drive back into the city. I'm going so slowly even though I'm doing the speed limit. But I arrive.

Driving home, back to my apartment with the white kitchen table and the grey chairs and the big windows with

low sills, I felt all the people in the cars around me. All their thoughts zoomed into me, their feelings. Some were late, and others were focused on seeing someone or getting to a store to buy some object or article of clothing. A cake pan. A warm sweater in a flattering colour. There were small feelings of hope and desire, and some deeper torments, too. One woman had been slighted by a friend in a public place. Another had been told by her sister that she didn't want to see her ever again. The feeling of not knowing why, the feeling of unfairness. Feelings of tightness, closing in, a tenseness. And then in another car, speeding into me, warm feelings of joy, a looking forward, anticipation. Good, good, good. All of it speeding into me—needles, a whirlwind acupuncture session.

And then, interspersed with these feelings, thoughts. *Remember to buy the can of tomatoes at the grocery store. I must invite Gloria over soon. I'm going to be late to pick up the children. If I don't visit old awful Aunt Lacy, she'll soon forget about me and write me out of her will. I have to get home and ice the cake. Chocolate or vanilla? Maybe sprinkles on top or strawberries? I must arrive home before the guests do. There is so much work to do how will I ever get it done I can't get it all done. My list is so long.* I hear this last one a lot. And there is hunger, too. The hunger of the body, and the hunger of the spirit, which is prevalent.

The hunger of the spirit is prevalent.

I've been waiting for a guide. Part of me expected that when I walked into my apartment, turned the key, there would be an angel sitting on my couch, waiting for me.

I walk in and stare at the couch. If I stare long enough the angel will appear. The guiding angel.

I am alone and I sit on the couch. I lean back on my wings. I wrap myself up in them. Oh, it's a lovely feeling.

My life is to be without plot. It will be ordinary and it will be a succession of ecstasies of becoming. I'm going to stand in one place and look at things—flowers, a leaf, the crumbs

on the saucer of a teacup—until I lose myself in the depth of them. In the early morning I'm going to take to the air right before the sun rises. No one will know because people only see what seems real to them, and even I know that I'm unbelievable, these wings, these feathers.

I know I must write this in a way that will have you question all of it, knowing that there are no answers. And still it must answer all your questions. Only questions can really answer questions. Breath answers for breath.

Writing this, I feel more alone than I ever have and sometimes I'm so bewildered just because I've written down words which will eventually reach *you*.

I don't understand at all why this is happening to me, but I also know that I'm not meant to understand. I'm meant to breathe and live, and beyond that, I'm meant to appreciate the beauty of things in a heightened way. This is the clearest understanding I have because I see the shapes of things and marvel, the colours and the scents of flowers and grass and the earth even. The beauty of music brings me to my knees.

It's so unceremonious. Becoming. I find this amusing. It's all so serious, but it's ridiculous, too. No one will ever believe how it is and why should they? I don't even want to be believed. I don't want to tell anyone how any of this feels. The only sane thing to do is write it down in this diary. Someone will find it one day and imagine they've found the scribbling of a lunatic. I'm a lunatic alright, I know I am, and happily. Isn't a lunatic someone who howls at the moon? Who follows the changing phases of the big eye in the night sky?

It's now that I look over at the plants on my windowsill and I see that miraculously they're still alive. All the African violets are in full bloom, and the ivy has made a path across the entire sill and crept all around the big window. The geranium is glowing red, and the hibiscus is full of pink blooms. The tree outside the window seems full and shakes its leaves at me, swaying a little in the breeze. The light coming in now is dappled and clear like vinegar or Perrier.

I have secrets now. I've not been the sort of person who has secrets. But maybe we all think we're open books, and there's no way anyone can be that exposed.

My dreams are now predominantly about flying. The dreams start with a walk down a forest path. It occurs to me that if I'm able to fly, it makes no sense to be walking. I hold the power of flight; I must use it. I do. I feel my cells alter; the frequency around me alters. I open the window to the sky, I fly through. I dominate the air; I am becoming the air. My body was made to breathe in this air, all of it, all of it. And it's glorious. As glorious as sitting in the perfect armchair, eyes closed, on a summer morning, listening to Mozart. And then a bird chimes in from outside the open window.

Or if you prefer, Vivaldi, Debussy, Ravel.

I'm writing this freely; I have no obligation to these words, or to anything but this gift I've been given. And yet I have no real understanding of what I've been given, I know that much. I keep expecting more. What I mean is I keep expecting someone to mentor me, someone to drop out of the sky and announce herself to me. How is it that one is given such gifts, and is then left alone? All I can do right now is go deeper. I have to mentor myself, follow what calls. I'm blundering forward, and it's a joy, but it's also painful because inevitably, I fall. But before I fall, such intensity.

In the late evening, I see a rainbow from my window and I go to it. Who wouldn't? It tastes like eating the most amazing cake—so many flavours, a sweetness, it is a dream. As I fly amid the wavelengths, I soak in the colours and the corresponding colours in my wings tingle and pulse in a kind of rapture. It's a lark, not the least bit serious; every part of me is joy, laughter, loveliness. Pure delight. I must have been smiling the entire time, playing as a child would in a fountain of water on a scorching hot day. When I return home, I am utterly spent. I lie on my bed and use my wings for a blanket, drawing my legs up and in, until

I am all wings, inside them. A most cherished warmth and comfort. I sleep so perfectly.

I keep reminding myself that this could all end. Why could it not? I've no idea why it began, so there must be every possibility that it could also end.

When I fly up into the tallest trees I can find and perch on the top of one of them, delicately, lightly, I remind myself, *this could be the last time. You must drink of this moment, deeply, deeply.* I close my eyes and take in the scent of the leaves breathing, the green lovely breaths. A bird brushes by, says hello. The breeze ruffles my feathers and I am wild and alive.

Early on I fell from the sky. I was too sure of myself. I fell and I must have looked like Icarus, if anyone had noticed, if anyone had painted me into the frame at all. I fell into a farm field and hid myself for a while in the haystacks. I'd forgotten for a few moments how to fly. I'd forgotten what I now was. That I had wings and they were by no means made of wax. I wasn't hurt and my landing wasn't horrific. I was like a bird that hits your front windowpane with an awful thump and appears for a while to be dead, but then suddenly and surprisingly flies away. I was somehow inexplicably saved, to fly again, to continue becoming. But if I hadn't, it would have been fair. I'd had my try.

It's morning now, and I stayed up all night looking out the window. It reminded me of my goal to become a poet. I used to think I knew what a poet was, but now I'm not sure. Poets are in a perpetual state of becoming and so am I, but does this make me a poet? Is it possible to forge myself into a new kind of poet? To be a poet in spite of the other things I'm becoming? Does it matter if the words I form into poems are not like the poems you find in anthologies? I think it's okay.

Everything will be okay. This is what I tell myself, and I think about what a good, sweet word is "okay."

It will be okay. I send that out. I hope it reaches those who need it. I transmit this on all channels, even the ones I don't yet understand.

We are often standing amid metaphorical ruins and rubble, but we are okay. It will be okay. I whisper this out to the universe, hoping that someone hears it. One person, even. I know how profound this simple sentence of encouragement can be. It's okay. It will be okay. You're okay.

I remember the words Cary Grant spoke in a movie, and that he often also signed his letters: "Happy thoughts, darling."

Happy thoughts, darlings. I send that out, too.

What I'm doing: reading over your shoulder in the dark. That's what I do now. I try to glean what sort of breathing I need to do in your presence. When I say *you*, I mean all the *you*s I have travelled to in the dark and the dusk. All the *you*s I feel in my vicinity and whose thoughts I feel, more than I take in word for word. You see, I've learned that it's necessary to mute the words, but the feelings come anyway.

I can see you reading your book, but the words on the page are strangely illuminated. Sometimes there is a lamp on, which overexposes them. And if the lamp has not yet been turned on, the words are floating in the dusk, and they too are difficult to make out.

Today I remember the story of Irene's angel. I'd forgotten it, caught up in the nuances of my own alterations and blossomings. I can't help but think of my wings as enormous bouquets of flowers that I've been given to tend.

Sweet orange tea roses, pink ranunculus, yellow poppies. Magenta peonies. Sunflowers. Deep purple anemone. Each petal is my responsibility. I know how delicate a flower is, and though my wings are like flowers, they are also like carved stone wings, immutable and strong, and they are also like painted wings, malleable and impressionistic. They are like fire, a burst of flames fed by pure oxygen. They are like

tree branches able to bend in a strong storm. They are like a painting born from a solitary, fragile dream laden with and soaring with time.

What I don't know is, will they last? Will they burn out? Or wilt, like flowers? Is there a shelf life to these wings? To me? Is it only a matter of time before I fly too close to the sun?

I continue to write this, even knowing that everything I'm experiencing is untranslatable. I find it like trying to translate a sonnet from Italian to Mandarin, having no knowledge of either language.

In between writing, I'm living. I have no choice. I continue. I open the door in the morning, and I leave, early, before dawn. I fly better at dusk and dawn, in the golden hour, when the sun is near the horizon. I don't know why. I see the auras of people more clearly, and I can fly closer to those who are calling for help or crying out inwardly. I look for others like me, murmurations of angels. Why is it that there are so few angels? I take off in the morning, and when I come back to my apartment after a few hours—still, no one. I sit on my couch and I await instruction. I sit in my room. Nothing, nothing. The silence is lovely, though, and I dive into it. Do you know how many strands there are to silence? How many kinds?

Solitude is not just a state of being; it's a companion, a thing to know.

A week passed. I was so sure that someone would come. That there would be instruction. I decided to go looking for someone who had the answers, someone who could tell me about this path I was on. I looked on beaches at sunset and amid the leaves in the golden hour on the tallest trees. I looked on hills, and I went all the way to the mountains. I tarried on the tops of tall buildings. I stood in line for the bus, I strolled through libraries, I went to the symphony. All for nothing.

I suppose I needed to be able to tell myself, *you are completely and utterly alone in this, Xaviere.* I needed to tell myself that as you would comfort and bolster a child with soothing words. *Everything will be okay, sweet girl, my pumpkin, my lovely one. You can do this, my child, my girl.*

I am a child in this, that much is true, but I am also a young woman. I need to get on with things. I decide that I must resume my life. Today I decide to apply for a job.

Xaviere
20 years later

I left this notebook empty for months and then years. In fact, I buried the first couple of notebooks, deep. After I had taken up residence in Irene's house. The pheasant farmhouse. I had written there for weeks. I had sat at her table, and I wrote everything. Then I wrapped the notebook in the white cloths that she'd left folded in a chest, cloths that must have belonged to him, the angel. I wrapped my notebooks, and I went to the hill where he must have left this earth, and I buried them three feet down. I planted a young tree to keep them company, my words, and when I went back later there was a strong tree, holding the hill. This tree of many wings.

I wrote things down for the first year because it kept me sane. It's time now to get some things down. It seems responsible, somehow. I'm responsible to whomever picks them up and reads them. *Hello.*

I thought being an angel would change everything, but it only makes my life more difficult. Some days are awful and some wonderful. Some days I just quit. But the next day I wake up, and the fact of my wings is indisputable. Well, they're disputable, all right. Just not for me.

I was going to be a poet. Instead, I became a librarian.

People want stories; they want books that have good endings, but they can't say what a good ending is. They want the plot to be exciting, not boring, and they want the next book they like to be like the last one they liked. The cover should be nice. The book should make sense and be easy but not too easy. It should be this or it should be that. People come in because they want a book, but other people come in because they're dying.

Everyone is dying. Does anyone care?

I have learned that angels don't have to be nice, only sometimes kind. But it's not a rule.

No one teaches you how to be an angel once you are given wings; you have them, they appear, but that is all. Rarely, someone notices them, and they'll say something that lets you know this. But you're so tired and they're so tired, and there are people all around, so you let it go.

I often imagine my life being made into a movie, like *Wings of Desire*, or the one with Meg Ryan, *City of Angels*. Angels are everywhere in the movies. But no one would want to watch a movie like this one. I'm not a superhero. Life is not like that. Life is so much quieter; everything is small, every act. There are no grand gestures or cinematic panning. One small thing leads to another small thing.

I thought angels would always be at peace with themselves. I thought angels were perpetually happy creatures. I thought there would be an aura of calm and a grave delight that would trail behind me. I don't really know how I come across. What I leave behind.

Here's the thing: I was given wings, and then I had to completely re-evaluate my purpose in life. But I could have done this without the wings. Without the ability to fly and hear things, and feel things right deep into my bones.

At the library, I don't pay any attention to the new-age books about angels. They seem to me to contain a lot of

guessing about the mysteries. Even I don't have the answers. Let a mystery be a mystery.

But I still look at paintings of angels in art books. Piero della Francesco's angels intrigue me. Chagall's angels. Leonardo da Vinci knew something.

There are poems, lots of poems, mentioning angels. They're hidden amid other poems. And that's really what it's like. We're all poems hidden amid other poems.

Every day when I'm working at the library, I take a book of poetry off the shelf and I find the poem I like best in the book. I leave it open on a table for someone else to read. Someone always reads it. I watch them from a small distance. I see them nod their head. Sometimes they close their eyes for a few seconds, or nod. Sometimes they will look left or right, wondering, perhaps, whose book this is, who was last reading it.

I try not to be too obvious. I only left Milosz's poem about angels out on a table just once.

> day draws near
> another one
> do what you can.

I set out Mary Oliver's poem, too, the one from the book called *What Do We Know*. She describes two angels in the poem "At Twilight an Angel." The first is in a garden. She says, "It's true, the wings are very beautiful." The second angel, though, appears in the middle of the night, hovers, is silent and unhelpful. The poet asks, "What, then, is their earnest business?"

Sometimes I set out a book of essays by John O'Donohue. He says, "One of the saddest losses that has come from disbelief in the invisible world is the loss of angels."

I'm not sure what my earnest business is. But the invisible world is one which I partially inhabit. There are some who don't seem to see me at all, and others who see me, but not my angel-self. I find this confusing.

What I do know is that when I see someone sitting in a chair staring into space, I stop and ask them if I can find a book for them. And they almost always say yes, perhaps because they wish to see what I'll bring for them. Invariably, they thank me and say, "You're an angel," or "Aren't you an angel?" or "You're my angel." I'm startled and, for a brief moment, I feel real.

If you can believe in dreams and also in poetry, then you have probably already flown. You have moved through the air and soared over the mountains with steel in your wings. Your wings have been black stone, and carved dense snow, and been covered with the finest moss, the sweetest small flowers. The believer of dreams and poetry and angels is a psychologist of flight, and the reasons you fly and the sensations you experience while flying and your subsequent lightness and intoxication will be the subject of the book you write after you read this one, darlings.

One day I plucked a book from the shelf, and I opened it to the idea that flight will conquer the world. "The world must fly," says Gaston. "There are so many beings which live by flying that flight is surely the next destiny of the sublimated world." And now I am tuned into the world of flight. I feel the wings of the dragonflies beating. The ladybugs, the common housefly. Millions of flying insects. Migrating monarch butterflies. Ravens, swans, flamingos. The world might be held in place by all the creatures who are presently airborne. Hundreds and hundreds of thousands at any one time.

Great blue herons, owls, and even vultures. Magpies, swallows, common sparrows, Canada geese. When I close my eyes, I can feel the effects of all the flapping, and it becomes a rhythm, a calm and soothing force, holding us all aloft, however earthly. It is, truly, our destiny to fly. It is so human.

At night, I'm not tired. In the summers, especially, I fly, I soar, to a library branch, not just the one I work at, and I watch the people go in and I breathe out the words, *do what you can*. The words are for me as much as they are for them.

When I go into work the next day, Elizabeth, my co-worker, will say to me, what realm did you visit last night? She's implying that I look as though I had too many drinks at the local pub. But she's right. Some days, someone will say, *look what the cat dragged in.* I smile. They all think I'm a big partier.

At night, in the summer, my wings meet the blue sky as if they were icing a cake. Smooth and creamy. I leave behind little peaks, swirls, curlicues, and stretches of delicious calm. In the cooler, crisper months, it's different. I don't feel the cold, but the air is closer and icy and flying through the flakes of snow is gorgeous. Every single feather tingles. When I lift off, there is the feeling that my wings are sparkling, as though they're giving off tiny sparks, points of electricity. It's joyful. Like the first taste of ginger ale for a child or champagne as an adult. It's a good, cheap and delightful happy all-the-way drunk, a sozzle.

I'm mostly invisible at the library. People are there for reasons and their minds are buzzing, humming, crackling, almost all of them. I can feel and hear the bubbling over going on in their heads even as I'm talking to them about a book they're looking for. Some of them, I think, see my wings for a moment, and then blink, and blink, until they can't see them anymore. They don't want to have to confront who I am or what they've seen. They don't want their errand to be thwarted. They need to stay on task. If I'm an angel, maybe they're an angel, too.

Every now and again one of my feathers, a small one, will give way. Angels don't moult like birds, but nevertheless, a feather will dislodge from time to time, and a new one will take its place. When the new one grows in, quickly, it takes me back to when I was coming into my angel being, back at Irene's place by the small lake. I have these flashes of what it was like, but sped up, like fast-forwarding through a movie you've seen before. The new feather emerges with a sharp, ecstatic needle-pain. My co-workers think I'm having a hot flash.

I take the dislodged feather, and I place it in a book I'm checking out for a patron instead of a bookmark. I do this when I feel that someone is particularly in need. Sometimes the feathers are very small, but they're vibrant, and they have a particular frequency; they hum. Each one is a message. An annunciation. It's always been this way.

And the message? I don't always know exactly what it is. It depends on who receives it. Usually the message is: there's more, there's something more. *You* are more. You have something within you waiting to be born.

You would think I would know. But I don't know the message, and I've no great insight into the great beyond. I can only tell you about the air I've flown through, the wings I've been given, about the joy of being alone and in silence. I can tell you that you're not alone in your confusion and your suffering.

Have I ever met another angel? That's something I'd want to know if I were asking an angel questions.

One thing the movies get right is that angels are drawn to libraries. I'm an old angel now. I don't think we live all that long. I've met three or four angels, each of whom has said they'd met one or two others. Maybe we're called. No one knows where. Being an angel means learning to be comfortable with the incomprehensible. I'm aware that this is also how it is for humans. Maybe everyone becomes an angel in the months before they die.

It's increasingly difficult to sort out my angel self from my human self. Am I no longer human? Just angel? The two are not so distant, is all I know. Was I always an angel? Do angels begin as humans or do they come into being at a random times?

The angels I met had no answers, only questions. This is what convinced me that they were my kind. One of the angels I met worked in a gas station on the highway, and another was a surgeon. Yet another worked in an ice cream

shop. All of the flavours, so many people seeking comfort. Each flavour seemed to symbolize a different sort of need for consolation. Chocolate is from the depths, very dark and warm. Vanilla is a favourite because it's quick, even if it is only temporary. It's soothing to both moral outrage and small disappointments. Strawberry is a consolation for slights of the past, long-ago painful and unresolvable episodes. No wonder shops have added myriad flavours, which answer a strong need for complicated emotions and their respective consolations. Butter pecan soothes the nerves before a performance. Cotton candy is consolation for childhood hurts that reverberate and awaken when a new hurt is felt. Rocky road soothes many bruises at once, and it is a balm for those hurts that were thought to be done with but rise up again unannounced. Tiger stripe is for the forlorn and inconsolable and is a comfort for those who have been made to feel powerless and meek. Mint chocolate chip is a comfort when one has to defer to someone with greater power, knowing that the powerful one has not given them the time of day or listened to them at all. Neapolitan is the trifecta of healing vibes, useful for when someone hurts so much they can't tell where the ache originates.

Though I don't always recognize them, I can hear the angel-ness in others' thoughts. I hear them in the thoughts of people coming into the library, wandering around looking at books, pulling out this one and that one. Some are sitting in chairs or at tables. I hear all the thoughts, a cloud of them. I take them in as a cloud, a cloud of feeling. Sometimes I sort them, sometimes I just take it all in:

> *Atwood. Grisham. Stephen King. Numbers, why are there numbers on all these books? What do they mean? I want a bottle of champagne and I want to stay at the Hotel MacDonald. She was kind.* Anne of Green Gables. *I just want a movie. She seemed safe. I don't want to be alone. I feel so alone. Someone just*

vomited in the women's room. I'd really like to watch all the Harry Potter movies tonight. Look at all these titles, strings of them, I just want Danielle Steele why don't they have Danielle Steele. Is that a girl singing opera arias in the bathroom so that they echo and carry? Her voice is astoundingly beautiful. What am I going to make for dinner tonight? If I don't leave now, I'll be late picking the kids up from school again. I just want to sleep. Why won't that person be quiet? I hate people. The smell in here is terrible. I should go outside. The news is horrifying. Where is the section about World War II? How am I expected to find anything here? I can't believe George died. What am I going to do now? What did the doctor say I had? Knitting. I want a simple book on how to knit. If I learn to knit my life will be so much calmer. Dogs. The funny one about the dog. I can't go home, I don't know what to do. He'll beat me again if I do. My feet hurt. It's so hot in here. Why do I never feel happy? What's wrong with me? I'm doing something wrong. If I could find another two dollars in my purse, I could get a cheeseburger and fries. That kid just ate a whole huge bag of Doritos. I'm so thirsty. What I'm looking for is the meaning of life. I mean there's a book about that, right? I really need to know. It's so confusing. I'm confused. Oh, look, this is just the book I wanted. I just need to sit for a minute. "I can't go on, I'll go on." Beckett, you know. Why can I never find Virginia Woolf on the shelf? I need to study. I have to force myself. At least 3 hours. If I don't pass this test, I'm a failure. Isn't this lovely, just browsing and finding so many nice things? I'd better hurry. Not much time, not much time. The doctor said this test is only precautionary. I'm not to worry, I'm not to worry. If only the sun would come out, I'd be happier. Oh, I can't wait until it's time to see Mike.

How do we know that we're not all angels? I never knew that I was one. Is one not an angel even before the wings appear?

I believe that perhaps the only reason I've been given these wings is so that I have to re-think myself. Re-imagine what I'm to be. To know what it is to feel separate from the human race while walking amid. And maybe I'm here to tell you what that's like.

The purpose of writing this is not to shatter any illusions you might have about angels. We're not that special. Being an angel is just being a guardian of daily life. There's nothing terribly sensational or extraterrestrial about it. I write this as a manual for myself, the how-to-be-an-angel book that I never received.

For a while I thought it might be a conflict of interest to be an angel and a poet. But of course it's not, for poets, too, are responsible for the entire world.

Am I getting blasé about my wings, about flying? On the contrary. It's a pure miracle that I get closer to and more ecstatic about. My wings are ever more powerful, but they're also more knowledgeable, having an intelligence all their own. They can communicate with other wings, unbeknownst to me. They've collected experiences, and know about winds, and currents, about temperatures. They know how to glide and pick up speed, and they are stellar at navigation. They're strong and they're supple. It's my wings that seem to have the instinct to know where to find those who are troubled. They carry me and gently set me down. When I would lose myself to the depths of blue, and when I would drink deeply and drunkenly of the intoxicating mists, my wings return me to myself.

My wings will carry me to gardens in the early morning before most people are awake. Maybe I'm vain, but I know how beautiful my wings look amid the rose trellises, the hydrangeas, the climbing vines—honeysuckle and morning glory. I revel in the lilies, the abundant greens, and all the colourful flowers—the marigolds, the dahlias, the geraniums, the masses of petunias.

The colours are juicy, and I drink from their auras, from the expirations and inhalations. A soft breeze and a small amount of dew in the morning is an ecstasy. What a darling pleasure.

The colours in my wings meet the colours in nature and reach out to them. They mingle and pulse, refreshed and energized.

My wings carry me to forests and mountains. Above the forests, the scent is green, and I'm filled with the breathing of moss and pine and millions of leaves. The sap of the forest rises up, and I meet it. The birds and insects are engaged in a brilliant choreography, and for a while I become part of it.

Next I fly to the mountains, making paths through them and around, but then landing on the tops. Feeling the stone beneath my feet, the icy-cold beauty, the texture of the blue-grey stone. I feel lightheaded and dizzy amid the pink clouds and the dark grey ones, but still my wings carry me; I'm not afraid of losing consciousness. I make contact with the mountain goats and all the high-altitude creatures.

I love flying in the morning, but sometimes I fly all night. I'm with the moon then, and the moonlight astounds me.

Do you remember when you were a child, driving with your parents at night, and the moon seemed to follow you down long and lonely country roads, onto the highway, and all the way back to your house, to your bedroom even? You'd lie in bed and gaze out the window, and there she was.

So now, flying at night, she's with me, round and lovely. Dependable. Whole.

I fly above houses; I perch on buildings downtown. But that's because I've watched too many movies, I suspect. The view can be very restful, and from a tall building I can contemplate my existence in peace. I used to be afraid of heights, but now I don't think about it, because of course, I can save myself. I have wings.

I read a lot because I don't need to sleep all that much. For a while I read theories about angels. They're all

different, so it's obvious that no one really knows what we are or what we do. I suppose many would be surprised that angels don't know the answer to their existence either. I'm searching for mine, even as I discover what my powers are. What is my reason for being? Is it enough merely to know that I am responsible for the entire world? What does that mean exactly? How far can I take it? I take it as far as I'm able.

Until I do make sense of who and what I am, I follow the calls. I keep people company, even though they don't see me. I'm usually invisible to those who call, which I don't understand. I look them in the eye and sometimes the eyes answer even if the person is unaware of me.

Sometimes I go to soup kitchens and have soup with the hungry. I can feel their hunger as I line up for my bowl. I try to sit by someone who is the most in need, who seems to be the least in need.

Was it Rumi, the thirteenth-century Persian poet, who said *try to be the person in the room who is the least in need?*

That is what angels do. Well, I shouldn't speak for all angels, but that is what I do.

I sit beside a man or a woman at the long tables, and we don't always talk. Sometimes we talk about the soup or the bread, or say, *could you pass the butter*, knowing that it's not really butter. Some days the soup is thin, or very salty to disguise the lack of flavour. At other times it's rich and thick. I don't know why this is any more than I know why wings were bestowed upon me.

As far as homeless people go, they are more likely to see my wings than most people. I think this is because of their true hunger. Not for meaning or for messages, annunciations. Their hunger at times goes deep into their guts and down into their legs, as though they have never once been properly fed. They are so thinned out and pared down they are practically transparent themselves. The hunger is for their ruined existence to be seen, for the beauty of the

wreck and their rage and defeat to be held up and understood and felt.

What do you need help with? and what is it that you love? Tell me something that you remember with joy.

"My dog used to follow me everywhere, and when I sat down, he would lie on my feet, and when I slept, in the crook of my legs. I had company."

"Darling, you are splendid," I reply. "You will be splendid again."

If you can get someone to remember a joyful moment, it humanises them, and we all want to feel human. Even me. But it's the rage, too, that we must sit with. It's the rage that is most real.

Even though I don't know why I'm here, I feel free. I know I've been given a gift. And when one is given a gift, freely, without obligation, it's a terrible sensation at first. We're taught to feel obliged when we receive, but this is quite the opposite. I owe no one anything. And yet there's a responsibility that comes with this kind of freedom. It's sturdy, because it comes from within. This, I realize, is the most wonderful part of the gift, this feeling of being responsible to others.

I'm not telling you everything here, not because I'm hiding anything, but because I don't want my life to resemble a novel or a quest or hero narrative. Neither am I here to write a memoir. A diary? Not that either. What am I hoping to leave behind? A photograph? Impressions, colours, a perfume. When you are in distress, or entering a deep sadness after a death or a departure, and you sit with those feelings, quietly and alone, sometimes you will feel a presence. That might be me. I want these words to be a sort of presence. Words are angels, too. You can't quite identify them, perhaps—it's something you want to say, but it floats away. Can't quite put your finger on the feeling even. You shake it off, you try to forget it. And it

will come back to you later like a dream. The memory of a dream.

That's all I can hope to accomplish with these words.

My writing becomes more disjointed as my life becomes a steady stream of thoughts and feelings of others. People want books that make sense, that are all sorted out for them, but life isn't like that, so why should books be like that? I'm not writing a book, though, so I can write what I like. Thank god for that.

The goodness of people can be quite overwhelming. I concentrate a lot of my energy on people who struggle with being good. They want to be decent souls but don't know how. They think they don't have the means. As though you need to be well-off to be good. But there are people who, though they also struggle, are purely good. In fact, the good people perhaps engage in more interior wrestling than most.

At first, I didn't seek out the good people at all. They didn't need an angel, I thought. I keep my eye on them. I leave them alone for the most part, but there are times when my presence is everything to the good person. The good people are never who I think they are, and they are also not usually who they think they are.

Yesterday a woman came into the library with a huge bouquet of flowers. She sat down at one of the long tables where everyone was studying. It was busy. A man was tutoring a young girl in math. A woman was reading *Hello* magazine with the royals on the cover. Another woman was studying English grammar. A boy was reading from a university textbook on geography.

The woman with the flowers was walking home from the grocery store and needed to rest for a while. She was fatigued. I brought her a glass of water. She didn't ask for it, and she didn't say *thank you* for it. I set it before her without saying a word. She drank it slowly, with great thirst. I admired her restraint. She answered my wordlessness with wordlessness.

From a distance, then, I noticed the quiet people studying at the table speaking to her. Remarking on her flowers. Asking to smell them. She offered them up. She passed them around. One flower was admired, and then another. A story was told. "When I was a child, my mother grew dahlias in our garden. She tended them so proudly," said one woman. "My husband gave me a red rose just like that one on the night he asked me to marry him," said another. "Those ones, what are they called? They've always been my favourite," said a man. "You have sure cheered me up with your flowers," said another. "Are they for someone special?" someone asked. "Yes," the woman said, "they are. They're for me." That made everyone smile.

The flowers were a light that everyone stared at. They were aglow.

The woman with the flowers stayed for twenty minutes or so after this. Quietly. Once in a while someone would glance up from their book and over at her, and smile. She seemed oblivious, but she wasn't. Not really.

The human angels intrigue me the most.

In the Library
by Charles Simic

There's a book called
A Dictionary of Angels.
No one had opened it in fifty years,
I know, because when I did,
The covers creaked, the pages
Crumbled. There I discovered

The angels were once as plentiful
As species of flies.
The sky at dusk
Used to be thick with them.
You had to wave both arms
Just to keep them away.

Now the sun is shining
Through the tall windows.
The library is a quiet place.
Angels and gods huddled
In dark unopened books.
The great secret lies
On some shelf Miss Jones
Passes every day on her rounds.

She's very tall, so she keeps
Her head tipped as if listening.
The books are whispering.
I hear nothing, but she does.

There are no strings attached to what I do. Some people find it hard to receive gifts, unless they're giving one back. My acts are not large. They are so small that hardly anyone notices and few believe. There is a moment I've heard people describe, when a book finds them, and occasionally one will even fall off a bookshelf and into their arms. Or they're walking by a table in a library, and a book will be sitting there and somehow catch their eye. Mere coincidences are rarely so.

You could say my life has been dedicated to arranging mere coincidences.

Writing this is like making an offering and wanting nothing back. Do you know how nourishing this is? To write without an audience.

As we know, not every story has a predictable plot arc. Many stories are not even stories but series of impressions. They adhere to no known set of rules. It's difficult to get a grip on such books.

There is a kind of writing that will live in the mistakes, the working-through of things, the muddling about. There is a kind of writing that is rough and beautiful and polished like a river stone, which lies at the edge of things and is only partly submerged. There is a kind of writing that is like a bird

you hear singing far off, and you can only catch part of its song, and you only think you know what species it is.

It's summer now, and the nights are very long. I sit on my windowsill and stare out at the sky. Many people have gone to bed, even though it's still light out. I can hear them breathing long and slow. I would like to tell you everything I know about loving the universe and how it's easier to love when everyone is sleeping. It's like a baby or small child who has been so much work, such a handful, during the day. The parent is frazzled looking after it, exhausted. All day long it needs this or that, it cries, it wants, it demands. But then at last, the child goes to sleep and the parent creeps into the room to watch it. Serene face, lovely, so beautiful and at peace.

The sleeping world is like this, too.

At the wind-up of some summer nights, each feather aches, I have flown so far and so hard. You wouldn't see me in the summer night sky, because I'm flying at such speeds, trying to reach everyone and every cry. Sometimes, as I walk amid the rows of books and tables at the library, it's just as intense.

I search for those who are holding their books as you would hold a child.

I am called to those who have everything at stake. Many people don't think about what that would be like. They lack empathy.

A family is moving out of their apartment late at night to avoid the shaming eyes of neighbours. Each of the three children carries their belongings in a garbage bag and a back-pack. The same goes for the adults, only the bags are fuller, larger. I hold the doors for them and help the children carry their stuff to the bus stop. They wait for a long time at that hour. I wait with them. I play with the kids. One of them sees my wings and touches them, smooths them as you would smooth long hair or pet the back of an old dog.

There is another side, I say to the smallest child. Do you understand? It won't always be thus.

I have an instinct for finding those moments that change everything. That moment that affects all the moments thereafter. It's the moment in a short story upon which everything else hinges. In a real, ordinary existence, it's not always easily traceable. But I am drawn to it, pulled, like the strongest magnet possible. When this moment is happening, my wings carry me there and I let them. I don't know why until much later. The smallest thing might affect the soul, the most intimate part of a person might be wrecked, and how they move from that circumstance is everything.

My powers are so extremely limited, there are moments when I wonder why I bother to exercise them at all. But in the end, it isn't a choice.

When I'm writing I don't look back at what I've written. I don't often think back to where this began. I keep looking forward because every day there is someone new to look after. A new small evil has revealed itself. Or a new sorrow, slight, a new betrayal or ache. Sometimes these are all easy to find, just within myself.

I'm on the side of life, always life. The beauty and joy of existing, and I'm not a martyr. I don't believe there is a value in suffering. It's not necessary to make a person stronger. Anyone who tells you that is trying to cover something up.

Just because I've spent my life without crying out doesn't mean I've been without need. But there are those who can manage without anyone answering. Without anyone discerning that there is a need there.

When I realized I was alone to figure things out, things became easier. Not easy. Just easier.

I remember going to a nightclub when I was younger. I'd had it with being a winged creature. If no one wanted to come and tell me why I'd acquired these wings, then to hell with it. I'd just be a regular person and rebel and go wild. What difference was I making, anyway?

I didn't try to disguise my wings. I wore my beautiful black tight cocktail dress and I let my wings have their way. It was like having a great hair day: my wings were shiny and in full plume. They were magnificent. Everyone wanted to dance with me and buy me drinks. It was dark and sparkly, and the music was out there, poppy and loud, and it was all bloody outrageous. I drank every drink that everyone bought me. Pink cocktails like flamingos, and green ones, and bright blue. One was red, glowing like pomegranate seeds. If I had lined them all up they'd have resembled the colours in my wings.

I was wild, but I wasn't necessarily drunk. I couldn't seem to get properly drunk. My bloodstream was no longer human.

Near the end of the evening a group of young men asked me which Victoria's Secret model I was. The really drunk ones could see the wings, but not everyone else could.

"What? No," I said, but no one believed me. It was absurd, I couldn't convince them. "I'm real," I said, wanting to burst this whole bubble around me.

They laughed and said how terrific I was and what an amazing model. "Oh sure, you're real, a real model. I've always wanted to sleep with a model." I slept with everyone and anyone. And the sex was outrageous and glorious and yes, fucking heavenly.

Other nights, I felt it was all foolish. I mean, Victoria's Secret? Me? I'd leave the club and regardless of who was standing outside in that shabby back alley with all the graffiti, leaning against the wall, smoking and flirting, I took off and up. I remembered what I was meant to do, to be. I flew. I embraced the air and the air embraced me. I was free of it all. Beyond thought. God, it was wonderful. It was the closest I've come to being drunk, but I was drunk on the air, the vibrations of the city that rise up and hover before moving off and drifting away.

I was drunk on being. On adoring. And I was drunk on existence. The air and the atmosphere are a miracle. We don't have to look around for examples of the miraculous; we need merely to breathe in and out, or move our hands through air, the wind.

As I move through the sky, I am unlimited. I dominate. I am filled with love and awe and wonder. But this is in me. I receive. I am full and the energy that surrounds me is magnificent. It's like swimming inside of a Max Richter composition. Modern and new and very old, at once. I fly from note to note, and there is a clarity. I'm in a fragile realm, but it's luxurious, fluid and velvety.

I can see why people portray angels with halos. When you commune with beauty, it begins to cling to you, great circles of gold. The word *angel* comes from the word for "messenger," and we know angels from paintings. Most of my ideas about angels came from looking at a couple of annunciation paintings in old art history books. The angel bows to Mary and announces her fate. And some of what's happening in the image continues to speak to me. The deep bow of respect. The acknowledgement of the beauty of another human being, the strength and endurance. The potential. Acknowledging the light in another being. Bowing to that light.

What I've learned is that it's not just Mary; it's every single person of every single background. It's not religious. It's a human connection. It's reverence, it's respect, it's acknowledging the holiness in us all. Each of us has the power to bless one another.

What people want, most of them? To love and be happy.

Why can we not listen better and tell people what they need to hear?

The discovery that the act of blessing someone is a kind of superpower.

What would I most like you to know about me? That I have known such freedom, which you might think of as

grace, bestowed upon me. A gift I accepted because I had no other choice.

For the most part I'm the most anonymous creature. No one thinks anything about me. They meet me and move on, and I'm used to that, I cultivate that. I'm from the invisible realm, subtle, intangible. Air clings to me from up high, bits of cloud and the debris of sky. When I leave the room, no one thinks about me. I know because I can hear what they are thinking. I'm clear.

I'm an improvisation. I walk into a scene and begin making things up. But I'm silent, so I don't disrupt anyone else's aura or frequencies. I know how to make myself appear completely ordinary so that I might observe others. What I observe is that not a single person on this earth is ordinary.

I'm traveling new territory, an inward territory so vast and so interconnected to others who are also traveling new realms. It's like that, you see: we are each explorers of ourselves, and instead we treat ourselves and each other like employees, or inconsequential beings.

And though I spend hours every day in an introspective state, I'm happiest when I'm looking outward, when I'm thinking about *you*.

It's not exciting, being an angel. It's tentative. It's gentle. It's like walking while the snow falls, big fluffy flakes. You're in it, and sometimes it's difficult to see through, but it's lovely and magical.

Being an angel is *little by little*. Being an angel is *henceforth*. It's the bluest blue you can imagine. It's the sound in the seashell. It's the laugh of the one you most adore. It's an answer and a question flooding in your mouth at once. It's a silence and an inwardness. It's as ordinary as birth and as miraculous as a new life brought into the world.

It's Rumi and it's Hafiz. It's a deliberate whirling and it's running by the ocean in the sand, sea spray in your face. It's the moment when you move from the heaviness of boredom to the glorious sparkling fizz of inspiration. It's seeing beauty and

feeling it in your pores and deep in the hollows of your stomach. It's that piece of music that sings itself into you. It's singing wild into the dark night in your car on the highway alone.

When I began my life as an angel, there were typewriters and cassette tapes. But now there are computers and laptops, and I sit on my couch with a laptop on my knees, my wings spread out behind me, and I lean on them. To be alone in the silence where my wings are neither holy or unholy is such a delicious dream that it allows me to say things from the darkest and most light-filled depths. I can travel so much further when I admit that even I don't know what these wings mean.

Part of me wants to lie and say that I'm writing with an inkwell and a feathered plume. I'm wearing long white robes, embroidered magnificently with a fine gold thread. I could be saying anything. I'm only trying to understand myself and to show myself where I've travelled. I'm learning how to arrange flowers. That's all that writing is, in the end: it's the invention of flowers, petal by petal. It's the invention of wings.

I've been with you all along, that's what I need to say.

People think of libraries as peaceful places, places where you can gather your thoughts and read and think. And this makes some people who are lacking an inner peace angry.

A man came into the library with a handgun in his messenger bag. He was filled with anger and calm, and each of those was frightening. He sat down in an armchair to plan, to gather courage. I sat beside him. I was ready to fly at him; I knew what I would have to do. His hand was on the flap of the messenger bag and he was going to open the bag and put his hand inside it, positioning it just so on the handle of the gun, his finger just so on the trigger.

This man had been deprived his entire life—of touch, of kindness—and he was filled with self-hatred. It was hard to feel and experience his energy alongside him, even for a short time.

I sat beside him and eventually gave him the book I was holding. He needed something to hold besides the gun.

He took it and cradled it in his arms like a baby. It was a large book, a heavy one. A big novel with long dream passages that you could live in and fly in and be held by. I said to him, "You can open it, you know." He finally did, after thinking about it for a while, as though he felt excluded from the space of the book. "Anyone can open it, you can open it," I said. He looked into my eyes at last, then at the pages of the book. He read the first paragraph.

We talked about the book and the author and what it means to enter the portal of a book, another world. He was very articulate. "It's been years since I looked at a novel," he said. Eventually he was ready to leave, and I asked him if he wanted me to take care of the thing he had in his bag. He agreed to it, and I reached in, twisting it, knotting it like the sculpture *Non-Violence* in front of the United Nations building in New York.

I hadn't known I had the power to do this sort of thing until then.

On another quiet afternoon there was a fight at the library. Two humans flying at each other, hitting each other in the stomach and face. When I arrived everything began to move in slow motion. I am unsure if time slows just for me or everyone. In books about angels or TV shows on Netflix, time slows for certain angels. I find it simply logical that an angel would have the ability to slow time.

The blood from one man's nose was in the air and then hit the floor. Sweat and blood were being knocked from each of them. I held my hand up and brought it slowly down. Otherwise they would hit each other until one of them fell, in that time-honoured manner, which I do not honour. And so they stopped. I walked toward the door and they followed me. Outside the front door I pointed west and one man walked that way. And I pointed east and the other man walked that way.

Two small boys watched everything from a distance. Their mother had dropped them off at the library so she could

go and have afternoon drinks with her friends. They drank vodka and water on ice so they wouldn't become dehydrated or consume too many calories. The small boys were looking at the ground where the fight took place; they looked at the blood and sweat mingling. They looked up with their impenetrable little smudged faces and saw me, and they took a step back because they could really see me now. "Will you read a storybook with me?" I asked them. "Yes, okay." And we moved somewhere nice and read books about lovely things and funny things. We read about monsters at the end of a book, paper bag princesses and wild things. We read about a cat who likes his shoes, a hungry caterpillar, and a leaf clinging to a tree.

Later they were walking home, after the library closed. They didn't know, but I followed them, flying above, quite high. I could see them get out their key and knew they were home. Safely. Safely home. Their home was safe but imperfect. But they were there.

Will I suffice?

I ask myself every day if I will. Often, when the question becomes heavy, I take off into the blue sky and let it answer. I fly with no attempt at plotting a course. I just rise and meet the blue with my own colours. I fly high, and then I coast on a stream of air for a while so I can think. I lie on my back and dream of what could be. I let the dreams come. I don't try and insist upon them or direct them, because dreams don't work that way.

Some people go home after work and wash up and go out drinking or to sing karaoke. They hop in an Uber and race off to the nearest bar. They hold their sins in their hands because those don't wash off so well. The river's too far away, so they drown themselves awake in vodka and Red Bull. Why shouldn't they?

I'm a being who has learned how to retreat into silence, and I know that the gift of the sky is a miraculous one. I

would wish for everyone to have the ability to rest on a cloud and sweep away thought, even just for an hour or two. When I come back down, I'm renewed, landing on the earth firmly again. It feels new and wonderful, too.

I'm an impossible being. I'm impossible. And yet I am. What could be more beautiful and inspiring than that?

The trouble is that the impossible will frighten some people. I must take care with those souls. But I take care of myself first. I, too, am real. I have hungers and needs, but I live in joy, which is the secret to life. What then is the secret to joy?

That is the question I want to give to people to hold in their hands like a small bird that is resting. And when the moment comes, they will know how to open their hands and gently raise them toward the sky, letting the heartbeat of the bird swell and rise and fly.

I'm free, but I'm also constrained. To whom am I obligated? I grew wings and immediately knew that I was responsible to the world. Which is too large, and yet I'm equal to the task. You might wonder what realm I exist in, but I exist in this one. I am in the realm of mornings, beginnings, revelations so quiet they come upon you and live with you all day before they dawn. I am in the realm of morning, which is a new flower, opening. I only want to understand the smallest things. I am in the realm of the infinitesimal.

I'm now going to reveal some secrets to you. (Here you might wonder if I'm addressing you, and I will say that if you are reading this, I address you).

The secret to being responsible for the world is that one begins by being responsible to ants. To a grain of sand. To a snowflake. To toast crumbs and biscuit crumbs and the larger crumbs of a blueberry scone. From there, you become responsible to bruises and small cuts. To the lump on the side of the head. You are responsible for falls and missteps. You graduate to hurt feelings, slights, forgetfulness, and cruel jests.

Eventually you learn to sit with loss, with despair, and with deep sadness. You learn to move from these back to contentedness, to peace, and even to moments of joy.

The tremendous gift of everything. The pain, and the roughness, too, are filled with an intense beauty, harrowing and brutal. Coming through things is where the beauty is, the cracks where the light gets in. In spite of the horrible. In spite of the unfathomable.

All that an angel is is someone who understands she is responsible for the entire world.

I have so few powers that if you have read thus far, I'm sure you must be disappointed. You have perhaps been interested in my wings and thought my ability to fly nice. But you've been waiting, waiting for some great revelation, some giant moment of consolation or comfort, for one grand feat that changed things so favourably and magnificently for someone. And maybe it's magic that you're hoping for most of all.

I like reading diaries better than novels, and better than watching movies. Diaries are life, you see. And life can be rather dull. Rather ordinary. If I have learned one thing, it is that the ordinary is more closely aligned with bliss and to splendour than what might be deemed spectacular.

The boy living in poverty whom I encouraged to do his homework after school for several years gets into college. The girl who was being bullied has a wonderful idea, and she becomes an entrepreneur.

The ordinary makes a difference, and that is why there is an aura around certain lives, certain small acts within a life. This is where we will find light emanating from an otherwise unconsidered thing or person. When the light emanates from a human being, we experience the moment that we suddenly know, knowing that we don't know what it is that we know, as a gift.

There are so many lives that no one would make a movie of, but they are worthy and lovely and real. My own life would make a terrible movie. There would be some glorious

flying scenes, but the rest of it is slow. I believe my life would make better paintings than a movie. A painting of me sitting in a library, listening. My wings could be visible; they would take up so much of the composition. My wings that no one sees. It would be beautiful if they could dominate the scene and remind the viewer that the world is full of such unseen mysteries.

Words are wings, too. Remember that.

I'm laughing this morning because I know it's near the end. My bones are thin and some of them are hollow, so this means that my life is thinner, too. Shorter. I'm not yet 60, but I know the end is coming soon.

Sophie Angela

The photograph was stolen on a winter day in Edmonton.

She was determined. She went downtown on the bus to the swirly art gallery building. She stopped at the fancy café named Zinc, with the blue lights, and ordered a drink. A dirty martini. When it arrived, she dipped her pinkie into it and dabbed behind her ears. Then she ate the olives and drank the martini in two or three gulps. Observations vary as to the number of gulps, but all witnesses say she dipped her pinkie into the martini and dabbed behind her ears. She was so quick that there was still snow on her boots.

The exhibition that she had come to see was on an upper floor, and she trudged up the steps in snow-caked winter boots. The snow ought to have been melting by now, but it wasn't.

The show was called *Snow Angels, Forgotten Angels, and Winged Beings*.

The exhibition began with the work of a graffiti artist who painted huge and colourful wings on the wall at the entrance. When you walked in you could strike a pose and have your photo taken with the enormous wings behind you. The wings were roughly painted, and the thick paint dripped down almost to the floor. It appeared to be still wet, still tacky to the touch.

After that there was a long row of Renaissance and baroque paintings borrowed from other institutions, many of them attributed to "Anonymous," or to the workshop of a more famous artist. In another room there was an angel by Anselm Kiefer, dark and burned and rising. There was a dress sculpture with decrepit wings by Louise Richardson. And a photograph by Francesca Woodman, where huge and crudely made paper wings hang high in a warehouse and before them is a woman, blurry, possibly jumping into the air like a basketball player doing a jump shot, very spirit-like. She's rising up into her wings.

There was a room devoted to Icarus, who wasn't an angel, but who had briefly known the secrets of flight. There were paintings by Odilon Redon and Marc Chagall.

There were movie stills from *Wings of Desire* on the wall, photographs printed very large, that the artist had then written all over in barely legible script.

There was an entire room devoted to Irene Guernsey and her photographs, and this is room to which she beelined. The snow was still on her boots when she arrived, and when she left there was a puddle left on the floor from the melting.

Who was she?

We don't know. She appeared on security camera footage briefly, at intervals. There was something wrong with the cameras this day that no one can quite explain. She was there and she was not there. We know she went up the stairs. There is footage of her standing in front of the photograph. And there is footage of a figure in a long coat leaving right after this, turning and walking out of the area. Later this same figure was downstairs and leaving the building. She had the photograph, in its frame, and because it is quite substantial, 40 inches square, she held it to the side with both hands. The photograph is behind plexiglass, so it's quite heavy, awkward, yet she didn't seem to strain.

Why did she do it? At first it was assumed that she had stolen the photograph of the angel in the falling snow for the

money. Museum curators expected to see it in the secondary market at some point. But years have passed, and the story has served to bring fame to Guernsey's work. So maybe that was the impulse, the impetus?

How does this affect everyone?

This is the question that intrigues me, that I wish to follow, am compelled to follow.

The thing is that events affect people you don't know, and they also affect people who might appear unfazed and entirely unaffected. Those things that make an impression on a person will be unremarked upon and internalized. Just one small thing can make someone change course or think about life differently. And that changes so much. Think of the butterfly effect—the idea that a butterfly flapping its wings in Brazil could set off a tornado in Texas. When a paper was presented at a conference on this topic, the butterfly was initially said to be a seagull, but friends of the scientist suggested that butterflies were more poetic than seagulls. Had it been called the *seagull effect*, this would have changed everything.

After the theft, the gallery hastily put up a frame, much the same as happened at the Isabella Gardner Museum in Boston after the big heist of March 18, 1990, when 13 paintings were stolen, including work by Rembrandt, Vermeer, Manet, Degas.

But the display of the empty frame as a reminder or placeholder and as an expression of hope that the photograph be returned is the only discernable likeness in the two crimes.

The show hung for four months. For one month the show was complete, and in the following three months, the empty frame became the centerpiece of the show, along with the tiny reproduction of the angel-in-the-snow photograph in a plexiglass stand not far from the frame. During the three months, the attendance at the gallery shot through the roof.

There were sometimes line-ups to get into the space and to pay for entrance to the show.

For the first month, before the theft, I sat in various places around the gallery. My project, as I designed it, was to record conversations, the overheard, and to observe. I would record what I saw and heard without intervening. When the theft occurred, there was a one-day closure, followed by an attempt to return to normalcy. When the interest in the media was so high, the empty frame was swiftly installed in the middle of the room on a plinth, and there was hushed excitement about the attention, along with the sombre and marginally calculated articulation of sorrow for what had been lost. At first there were a lot of jaded comments. Some ventured that it was all a publicity stunt designed for Instagram. And it's true that many people who visited positioned themselves behind the empty frame and artfully arranged their poses and facial expressions to appear angelic or sad.

After the theft occurred, I usually sat near the frame, on a black faux leather bench, and pretended to be drawing, or rummaging in my purse, or thinking deeply. I listened. I wrote. I might have appeared a quaint figure, as someone who was writing a book in a movie would look. It was my idea to emulate the project at the Isabella Stewart Gardner Museum in Boston. This is where the French conceptual artist Sophie Calle created two projects after the notorious theft of thirteen objects from the museum in 1990.

My name is Sophie Angela Duras. My mother wanted to name me Angela, and my father insisted on Sophie. "Being named *Angela* is too much pressure to be good," he said, and she said, "And *Sophie* means 'wisdom,' so what kind of pressure is that?" "Everyone should have that pressure," he said. As for me, I'm not sure if being an observer, a listener, is any indication of wisdom, but I've always been drawn to the idea of angels. For some people, their name is their destiny.

Maybe it is for me, too. I can't help but think that my name has something to do with Sophie Calle, even if my parents had never heard of her.

She was the artist in residence at the Isabella Gardner Museum in Boston.

After the thefts, she had curators, guards, conservators and various museum workers stand in front of the empty frames and talk about what they remembered about the stolen art. Absence and memory were the themes of the piece Calle created from these interviews, which was titled "Last Seen." Then in 2012, she revisited the project with "What Do You See?" where she questioned the museum's staff again, in the Dutch Room from where many of the paintings had been taken, but without referring to the missing work. Everyone talked about the missing work anyway. The absence was deeply felt.

For the show at the Art Gallery of Alberta, inspired by Calle's work, I began by merely recording what I heard. What I saw. I arrived at the gallery as though I were going to work. I brought my lunch, and I bought a coffee at the small kiosk outside the room I sat in and drank it at one of the small tables in the atrium as I watched and listened to the people coming and going. But mostly I inhabited one of the long black leather benches, the kind that is ubiquitous in such places. I sat with my notebook out and I sketched people when they were too far away for me to hear them. Sometimes I stood up and walked around. I tried to get closer to people so I could eavesdrop.

Some people talk loudly, and others speak as though they are in a library from the past, where people are shushed if they speak.

I have repeatedly heard what I will call a spiritual cry. A person alone, usually but not always, and from across the room, a crying out. A thin guttural expression that is pure feeling and seems to take the person by surprise. It pierces. Then disappears into the air so thoroughly you wonder if you really heard it. Was it a howl?

There are people who talk not at all. I record their movements, their stance. I'm the sort of person who puts her hands, clasped, behind her back when she looks at a painting, and there are those who do this as well. There are those who stand for a very long time with one arm folded across their chest and the other drawn up to their face, hand on chin, finger across cheek. There are those who use the power stance, hands on hips, feet positioned a little wider than shoulders. There are those who take steps in, and then back up, and then step back toward the painting again.

Larger works require different movements. Some people walk back and forth. Some move quite far back, before coming in to examine various parts of the painting closely, intently. It seems they are looking for something in particular, but it's hard to tell what.

From my position in the room of the empty frame, I can see into two other rooms, at least partially. I am able to observe people looking at paintings in each of those rooms and note their movements, which are a sort of dance before each painting, and how they look at the brushstrokes. It's different with photographs. The viewer doesn't interact quite so much, not at first. The gestures are smaller.

I believe in recording the smallest exchanges in human life. They tell us something about ourselves in ways that epic novels do not. I'm on the side of poetry, you could say. But perhaps I'm also aligned with the scientists who observe the behaviour of tiny organisms in their increasingly miraculous microscopes.

Am I an artist myself? A writer? Okay, yes to both, but I don't want to feel confined or labelled. I suppose you might think of me as an affect artist. I'm interested in how an event or object or encounter affects a person, and then how that affects, in turn, other people.

Overheard:

I wonder how she did this without Photoshop.

But mostly people don't wonder, at least not out loud. Not about how the image was made. I heard them ask, *Why this one?*

The missing work leads them inward. The missing work becomes a work unto itself. The absence, a thing.

Once in a while someone strikes up a conversation with me about the empty frame, the missing art work. And then they begin talking about themselves, their own encounters with angels, the emptiness they sometimes feel inside.

Muriel walked in by herself and she hesitated. Most people naturally turn left when they come into the room, and circle around, looking at each photograph in order. She resisted this. She wanted to go right.

She was wearing a navy-blue suit and a bright pink scarf. She wore low heels, navy and white. Perhaps most remarkable is that she wore a fashionable pink hat, which isn't something people usually wear in this city. We're known, generally speaking, in Edmonton for dressing down, for being inconspicuous. For taking pride in not looking like we're fashionable. It's a working-class city, and no one admires a show-off. The hat, though, suited her perfectly.

She went to the right when she entered, but then veered off and began looking at the photograph across the room. The one that had been found in Irene's house but was inconclusively not by her.

It was the one titled *Xaviere.*

When she finished, she came and sat on the bench, perched on the end, as though she were about to jump back up at any moment. The gallery was empty, just the two of us.

Over her shoulder she said, "It's hard to believe she's from here. Guernsey."

"Do you like her work?"

"Oh, yes, I'd never heard of her until I walked into the room just now. That's how we are here, isn't it? Oblivious to our own."

"Yes, I think it is, really."

"And the subject matter, so unlike us."

"Ah, yes. Yes."

She stood then and looked at every single photograph with great concentration. She left her handbag on the bench beside me, which I took as a substantial gesture of trust, though it could have been related to her health condition. She had just had some news. And it was not good, she said. I didn't pry further.

A young man was wearing faded jeans and a t-shirt. He carried a leather jacket, holding the collar, so it almost dragged on the floor. As he looked at the paintings and photographs, he was perfectly still, and when he finished and was ready to move on, he shrugged his shoulders. *Huh*, he would say, then move to the next one. It was as though he'd absorbed what he could absorb, as though he'd discovered some truth, and then as it came to him, he uttered: *huh!*

Quite often people browsing the gallery would be having conversations entirely unrelated to the art. They were making business deals, discussing friends or family members. They were gossiping. Talking about what they did last weekend. What they wanted to do next weekend. What someone had done in the office.

I began asking viewers if they would give me their phone numbers so I could call them up in five years and ask them what they remembered about the art show they had just seen, and some of them said yes. I had them write their names in a small white address book. I gave them a pencil, and they printed their names and phone numbers in the tiny space provided.

I wanted to see if they were still thinking about the show in the future, I told them. "I doubt it," many of them said. "And I might not even have the same number. I might not even be alive." *Let's be hopeful*, I replied. *I will talk to you in five years*, I encouraged.

I overheard stories of encounters with angels. I heard people say, "It was just like that. I was in the forest and I was a small child, maybe four years old. I'd wandered off and gotten lost. I heard later that my family had spent two hours looking for me. We had been camping by a lake and some trees, and I was chasing squirrels, or a bird. At some point, I wanted to get back to the campground, to our tent, but in getting back I must have moved further away. Something told me to sit down. Something sat beside me on a fallen log near a path. And that's where my parents found me. My mom said she remembered thinking someone had their arm around me, that she had seen a winged person beside me for a split second. It was a hallucination, she said, that came out of her fear and then relief at finding me. But I knew what she had seen was real."

And this other thing started to happen. One day, one person would be talking about an angel encounter, and then several days later, another person would come in and relate something similar from a different viewpoint or angle.

"I was in a car accident on a secondary highway late at night. I'd been drinking. I admit it. I rolled my vehicle and when I woke up, I was upside down in the ditch. I probably should have been dead. I thought maybe I was. I might have been. An angel came to me and helped me exit the car. So gentle. I never fell; she held me, and then I lay on the grass as the sun came up in the morning and she walked across the field toward the sun and disappeared into the sunrise. I kept staring at what looked like wings—colourful, glorious and spellbinding."

"Do you think it was real?" I asked.

"I don't know. But it felt real. So maybe it was as real as anything else."

And then a day later, I overheard a woman talk about seeing a car crash and pulling over to help. Seeing a figure take someone out of a car, lay them on the grass, and then walk away into a wheat field drenched in the morning sunlight.

There were similar details. The person had seen wings and they were so colourful, she had been transfixed and completely forgotten about the injured person for a bit. "I kept trying to name the colours in my head, there were so many and so many hues and variations. I couldn't keep track, but I couldn't seem to not try. And then the EMS vehicle came with its lights and sirens, and everything swam out of my head. As though it were a dream scattering upon wakening to an alarm. Just the scent of it left."

I invariably asked people if they had ever seen an angel. One response: "Of course I've seen an angel, I remember seeing one, but I always feel like I'm lying if I tell you that I've seen an angel because I'm not sure. Maybe I'm remembering a dream. And when I tell the dream, each time it becomes different: more real, but also less real. It was a dream."

There was a lot of doubt being expressed, which I found interesting. There was doubt, but that doubt was mostly brushed aside. Acknowledged and brushed aside. Or it was held onto as part of the experience.

If one expresses doubt, then, one neither believes nor disbelieves, but is in a medium realm, and one is able to jump easily to laughing the whole thing off.

Does it matter if there was an angel or not? The experience is real, the doubt is real, the wondering is real.

The experience becomes part of our personal story, even if it's only a feeling. We can carry the moment of not-knowing with us pretty far.

Some visitors to the gallery had been to the show before the Guernsey photograph was stolen. They came to see the empty frame and spent an inordinate amount of time with it. They spent much more time with this empty space than they did the rest of the work in the exhibition.

Some people notice the frame and remark upon it to their companions. Some must touch the frame, despite the sign that says not to do so. You can hear them say things like, "It's not as though it's art, is it? I can touch it if I like."

The frame chosen is not the original frame from the photograph, as it was stolen along with the work of art. The frame is one chosen to represent the fact of the disappearance. It is not what I would have expected; it is quite extravagant.

Even though there is a small reproduction of the image of the stolen photograph, the angel in the falling snow, many people who had seen the show before the theft spend time trying to remember it.

For first-time visitors, who came because of the attention brought to the show because of the theft, the curiosity is of a shorter span. They squint at the reproduction. "Why would anyone want to steal that?" is something I often hear. "I don't understand what's so great about it that someone would want to steal it."

One young woman came into the gallery and stood in front of the empty frame for some time. She had tears in her eyes. At one point she wept. She took a tissue from her purse and dabbed at her eyes, then her nose. She sat beside me. "Are you okay?" I asked. "No," she said. "But I'm fine. Thank you for asking." We sat in silence for a while before she said, "I was here before and this group of photographs has meant so much to me, you see. They've made me remember things about myself and reminded me to love myself in spite of everything. I don't know why they have, but they have. Also, when I look at them, it reminds me of how little I actually know, about how we see ourselves in the world and what we miss."

Another pause.

"Does that make sense?"

"I think it does."

I listen and catch parts of conversations:

"Where do you think she got the feathers from? How did she make the wings?"

"Well, it's an angel, isn't it?"

"Angels aren't real."

"Yes they are."

"How do you know?"

"Well, I've never told anyone."

"I think she collected the feathers and constructed these wings with glue and maybe cardboard and some wire. And then she shot the photos in low light or something."

"When I was eight and my mother died, an angel came to me."

"Children are so susceptible to that sort of thing."

"But the thing is, we weren't churchgoers, and I don't think I'd even heard of angels to that point. I didn't have a word for it yet. I'd never heard the word, *angel*. And I'd never seen a picture in a book or anything. I'm sure of it. I remember afterwards seeing a picture and saying to myself, oh, that's what I saw that morning after my mother died."

"Maybe it was your imagination. It was grief. The way that things manifest."

"It was something else."

"Even if you did see an angel, *these* aren't angels."

"How do you know?"

"Why do I want to know?"

"Excuse me?"

"If they were angels they wouldn't be in photographs."

"I don't know about that. I mean, they seem real to me."

"You're an expert on angels?"

Sophie Angela
Everything Affects
Everyone

Asking the proper question is the central action of transformation—in fairy tales, in analysis, and in individuation. The key question causes germination of consciousness. The properly shaped question always emanates from an essential curiosity about what stands behind. Questions are the keys that cause the secret doors of the psyche to swing open.

—Clarissa Pinkola Estes

There was a photograph in another room that I haven't mentioned until now. It's by "Anonymous." A roll of film was found in Irene Guernsey's house, but it was not shot by her. It wasn't a type of film she ever used. There was, apparently, a note folded up and rolled into the canister with it. And the note said, *My name is Xaviere, and these are photos I have taken of my new self. I am exactly as I have always been.*

I mention this here because it comes up quite a lot when I talk to people about the missing artwork, the stolen photograph. The curators titled the photograph *Xaviere*.

Five years have passed. I take out my small white address book, and I begin to call the numbers of the people who viewed the art show with the empty frames. I put the same question to all of them. How did this affect you?

Gwen S. said, "Everything affects everyone, doesn't it? I went to view the show where I met you because I'd heard about the art theft, the theft of the photograph. I hadn't known there would be a show at all, of angels in art. It made no sense to me. Why would anyone want to go to see a frame with nothing in it? But I did want to see the angels, and it was the empty frame that drew me. Who knows why. I think it speaks to the void in all of us. And you could put your hand right through it, you could reach into the nothingness. I needed to do that at that time, I guess. I have a real memory of reaching my hand in, as if into the wardrobe that leads to Narnia. A coldness, you know? But magic. As if my hand had been somewhere, travelled. Into the threshold of the unknown. That was all, but I thought about it for a long time after. Or maybe, it's more correct to say, I just felt those feelings I had at that time. That experience stayed with me. I haven't really tried to analyze it. It's not the sort of moment that lends itself to that, is it? At least I don't think so.

"Sorry, what was it you were asking? How did this affect me?

"I find myself thinking back to that show quite a lot. It was overwhelming, just the deluge of angel images. So many of them. It felt wonderful but so unreal. I don't believe in angels, but there are so many in art. I couldn't believe that someone from here, from Edmonton, could fit into that show.

"And there was that one anonymous photograph, you know which one I mean? I think about it every day. The way it was in grainy black and white, and yet it made you feel so many colours. The angel was neither here nor there. When I looked at it, I felt inhabited. By the angel? I guess so. I was lifted up with her. I didn't want to be set down after. It was transporting.

"To answer the question, in the five years since I gave you my phone number, a few things have changed in my life. I've even wondered if giving my number might be the catalyst, rather than seeing the angels? Knowing that I'd be asked something about them years later. That there would be a follow-up of some sort.

"My mother died not long after I saw the angel show, the empty frame, and I was with her the whole time. I mean, really with her. We hadn't spoken in years. We talked a little bit, but we never really said anything. I'd send her birthday cards and I'd check in on her from time to time. But it was always about the weather or other small talk. I told her about the show and was surprised that she wanted me to describe it in detail. We had long talks about the empty frame, what that signified. She got pretty philosophical.

"*There will be an empty frame when I'm gone*, she said, *and maybe I'll appear in it as an angel from time to time.* I'd never heard her speak like that. It was a comfort. We talked a lot about absence. She said a few things to me that I hold onto and always will. She gave me what I needed to hear. She said she knew she wasn't perfect, but she loved me. That changed a lot for me. After that, I was able to forgive."

Marcus G. said he'd never once thought of angels. His then-girlfriend had dragged him to the art gallery. She had thought the show stupid, though.

"I went with some reluctance," he said. "And she ended up saying things like, *Oh, this is too much. Too many angels. It's saccharine,* she said. And I replied, *Yes, it is.* I acted

nonchalant. But I felt it, you see. Something happened to me. I'd felt alone my whole entire life. I won't get into it, but I wasn't loved as a child. I don't know who my father is, and my mom, she was drunk or on drugs most of the time. I don't remember what she looked like without a cigarette hanging from her mouth. Anyway, looking at the art, something cracked in me, and I tried hard not to show it. I think I managed it. She didn't know. But I went back another day, too, without her, and just let the images sink into me.

"I realized my girlfriend, well, we weren't compatible. I suddenly had this other idea of what love was. What it would be like to love someone else, to want to look after them. I wanted to be caring. I wanted to be of use."

What are you doing now?

"I'm working with at-risk youth. It's something I'm called to do. And I think I make a difference. I hope I do. One of them was having suicidal thoughts last night, and I convinced them to live."

Julia R. said that after seeing the angels she let go of certain people, and that has made all the difference in her life.

"Once you've said things aloud about someone, it's difficult to go on being friends. They feel it, don't they? And I felt that this person had said things about me, and to be honest, I had also voiced things that I didn't like about her. So why go on being friends?

"We had stopped accepting each other, forgiving each other, and witnessing each other's lives. And I couldn't go forward with her, but recognizing this in myself was useful. I don't know if it had to do with seeing the empty frame, or the angel show, but I do remember going home after, and thinking that I really needed to sit down and evaluate my life. Like, *Am I contributing? Am I a good friend to the people I love? Am I a decent human being?* And I thought, *No, I need to be better, and I need to surround myself with people who inspire me.* This all sounds very Oprah or something, I know, but it's real. I'm better at accepting my own

faults; I'm better at accepting people as they are. I'm less fatigued by relationships, because I'm more open, I think.

"Looking at that black-and-white image of the woman who looked like she'd just emerged from a damp cocoon… that haunts me. She was surprised, you know, but triumphant. There was a weight, as though she'd settled into her body. And I wanted that for myself. To settle into the core of my being.

"It sounds like a simple enough thing, but to that point, I hadn't thought of that as a goal. I hadn't thought of goals in that way at all, even. I wanted to be myself, I wanted to be that evolved.

"I sought that core of silence and steadiness within. Some people spend their whole lives without that feeling."

Georgia M. said that after seeing the art exhibit she started noticing things. "It made me realize that there were things that are there if we attend to them. All of these artists painted angels, or found angels, and who's to say they didn't see or feel them? For me, it wasn't a question of belief in angels, but it was about a willingness to see what *is* there, and to witness the world with a deeper awareness. But also, to be open to the unseen world. By this I mean, attending to all we don't know, can't see. The thoughts that swirl around a body. The unknown experiences and feelings of strangers."

Roxanne L. said, "I remember that that day I had a compulsion to fill that empty frame. I wanted to put the grainy black-and-white photo titled *Xaviere* into it. I thought, *What would the harm be?* And anyway, since then, I've had this recurring dream where I do, I take the one photograph off the wall and I put it into the frame. Of course, in the dream, it fills the frame perfectly, just like the shoe fits the princess in 'Cinderella.' It's a perfect fit. I keep thinking, *Why didn't the thief take this photograph?*

"How did seeing the angel exhibition affect me? It affected my dreams. That much is certain. And in turn, my dreams

affected my waking hours. I realized that I could rearrange things. Slowly, I've been filling the empty frames in my life. I began seeing a counsellor. I began going for long walks. I'm healthier. I know who I am, or at least I'm closer to that. I know that glory of being myself. I'm coming close to saying to myself, *I love you, too.*"

Oscar L. was reluctant to speak to me at first. "Yes, I do remember you. I remember the show. That's not it."

"Take your time," I said. "I understand if you don't want to talk about it."

"Maybe that's what I need—understanding. Because things happened to me after seeing that show, and I don't understand how, but I think they're connected to what I saw, what I felt. I remember when you asked me for my phone number so we could talk about it in five years, and I gave it to you just to get rid of you, quite honestly. Afterwards I thought I should have given you a fake number. And then I said to myself, *Well, you'll have a new number in five years anyway.* Something has made me keep this number, even though I've changed phones.

"What I realized is that it's okay to look out for people, to feel responsible for them. To look them in the eye and say, *I can help you.* I started to figure out how to make someone else feel safe. And maybe this is why my son came out to me. It was hard for him. He thought I wouldn't accept it. He was surprised when I did. I told him it wasn't easy for me, but at the same time it was the easiest thing in the world. He's my son. Of course I accept him. If this had happened a year earlier, I don't know if I could have. So when you ask me if I was affected by seeing all those angels, I guess I have to say I was. And I reject the possibility of an empty frame when it comes to my son. I want him in it."

Ashley Y. said, "I took the angels to heart, I really did. And then I just couldn't stop looking for them. I watched all the

movies I could find about angels. I've watched *Wings of Desire* so many times. I've watched Meg Ryan in *City of Angels*. I'm interested in the angels that want to become human."

Mirabelle S. was one of the last people on my list to phone. Her number was unreachable. Perhaps I had written it down incorrectly. But on the same day that I had set aside to phone her, she phoned me.

"You said five years, and I put it on the calendar. I expected you to call yesterday, and when you didn't, I looked you up and found your website. You probably shouldn't put your number there, you know, but I'm glad you did. There are things I want to tell you. Because after viewing the angel show I felt accompanied. And because of that I started to speak out. What I mean by that is that when something didn't feel right, I said it. When someone looked down on me, or belittled me, I spoke out. And gradually, I began to do this for others. I was kind. But I didn't back down. It wasn't calling people out. I asked them questions. Are you sure you want to be saying this to me, in this way? Are you sure you want to use that tone with me?

"And so one day, I got an email from someone saying my mode of questioning had changed her life. I had helped her stand up to a bully, and this had had repercussions. She left an abusive situation. And now she helps other people leave abusive situations. She said to me, you have no idea how what you did now affects so many others. The ripples, she said, are far reaching. I have saved babies, small children, from terrible circumstances. I have saved women from beatings and unspeakable violence. You have had a hand in this.

"This is how seeing the show of angel pictures, on that one day, has affected me. Realizing how one small thing moves outward: it moves in mysterious and mainly unknown ways."

Dora L. said that she will never be the same. "I am changed forever. I still don't believe in angels. But I spent

that morning in the art gallery looking at the way other people reacted to them. So many of them glowed. They were basking in the presence of all these inventions of wings. For me, the wings are a metaphor. And a symbol of hope. We can lift each other up. Some of us can fly. We can be buoyed. I looked then at the colours in the painted wings, and the details in the photographs. When I came to the empty frame, I said to myself, I can fill that frame. We all can. I can be an angel for you."

I attempted to ask the proper question. How did this affect you? And the best answer is that everything affects everyone. I recorded the answers I was given. And then I published them in a small book which I titled *Everything Affects Everyone*. Between each response, I had a page that just repeated those words. Everything Affects Everyone. If I had been braver, the book would have just been pages of just that phrase.

Michelangelo and Antonia

Preface

I'm Antonia Green, and I met the actor Michelangelo Dupree in April of 2018. She had come to Canada to research her role in a movie that she will be writing and starring in based upon the obscure life of Irene Guernsey, the photographer of angels, whose work had been recently discovered, or perhaps rediscovered. She found the place where Irene had lived, and which is where I now live. I invited her in, having no idea who she was, or how famous she is. I think she found this endearing, or at least refreshing. We had spoken several times before she told me she was an actor, rather than someone merely researching Irene. Of course, I knew quite a bit about Irene, as I was also researching her life, because I'm writing a book about Irene.

In a way, we were competitors, each wanting to tell the story of Irene in our own way. But we each decided early on that we were meant, instead, to be collaborators. When Michelangelo suggested that we sit down and record our conversations, I agreed.

The art theft had alerted her to the existence of Irene Guernsey, and she wasn't the first person who had

knocked on my (also Irene's) door. But Michelangelo was persistent. She felt that this house was some sort of key to knowing Irene. And obviously, I felt that as well, since I was living in it. I liked Michelangelo as soon as I met her, and I brushed away the feeling that I had met her before. She seemed so familiar!

Because I was quite ignorant of Michelangelo Dupree's fame, at least at first, we were able to talk as two artists. We spoke as equals. I want to be completely honest and say that when I did find out just how well known she is, this changed things, at least a little bit. I'm only human, and while I'm not easily impressed by such things, it was impossible not to be affected by her stature. But then, over time, we slipped back into our initial mode. She put me at ease, and I would forget for intervals that she had this thing called *fame* that she carried around with her. She wasn't reluctant about it—she embraced her fame—but she also knew that she, too, was an ordinary person. She was, and she wasn't.

Perhaps this, though, was why she was so interested in angels, in Irene's ability to commune with them, to see them, to find them. To live the angels.

Our mutual interest in Irene, the art theft, and, I suppose, this idea of being ordinary and largely unknown connected us, and because we wanted to negotiate our mutual interestedness, we decided to record our conversation on our phones, each of us on our respective phones. This way if one malfunctioned or lost its charge, or there were technical difficulties, we would have a backup.

This was after I had discovered who she was and had Googled her. We didn't have any idea of sharing the conversation, or transcribing it, or podcasting it, or disseminating it in any way. We simply wanted it for ourselves. She, because perhaps she would look back on it when her movie was being made or scripted, and me, because I thought it would help me sort out my thoughts on the book I was writing, or making notes toward.

So what lies ahead, for any reader, is a somewhat self-indulgent, but mainly unselfconscious exploration by two women who, if I'm not overreaching, find each other interesting, and even extraordinary.

Michelangelo: Let's maybe get this out of the way, first, because say someone comes upon this conversation someday, they might need to know how you had no clue who I was when we first met. Which I suppose makes me sound a bit full of myself, but the fact that you didn't was extremely helpful in all sorts of ways. And it should be said that I didn't attempt to disguise who I was.

Antonia: [Laughs.] No, you did not, and I'm a little embarrassed still that I didn't recognize you. Well, it was more than not recognizing you, I hadn't heard of you. But I'm not particularly attuned to pop culture—not out of any disdain, mind, but there's so much of it, and I suppose I'm old. [Laughs.] And then when I Googled you, well, I'm sorry. You're very famous, as it turns out.

M: But we were able to get to know each other before you knew that, and that was really lovely for me.

A: People change, I'm sure, once they know who you are. Or they can't quite be themselves. I'm sure I have, a little, too. I mean, I've tried not to, but your fame is quite a powerful force. You're larger than life, regardless—I felt it when we met, but didn't immediately put my finger on that, so to speak. There was something about you.

M: Well. There was something about you, too.

A: No!

M: Honestly, yes.

A: Okay, so let's say who we are and talk about our names for a minute. I'll introduce you. I'm talking to Michelangelo Dupree, the actor, who has played the roles of gritty detective, fantasy queen, Edwardian upper-class woman, and most recently a homeless woman who won the lottery, a role that has garnered awards buzz and critical acclaim. She is currently

researching the life of Irene Guernsey, the reclusive and little-known photographer, whose picture of an angel was stolen in an unsolved art heist at the Art Gallery of Alberta. Michelangelo was named after the Renaissance artist, and so we have an interesting thing in common there, don't we?

M: Well, yes, we do, because you were named after the artist's apprentice, weren't you?

A: I was. There was a note found after the death of Michelangelo, the artist, and it was addressed to Antonio, his apprentice. The note said, "Draw, Antonio, draw, Antonio, draw and do not waste time." My parents read that in an Annie Dillard book and liked it. Because I was a girl, they named me Antonia.

M: And do you draw?

A: It turns out that I don't draw, but I write, which is not entirely unlike drawing. And so I often tell myself, *Write, Antonia, write, and do not waste time.*

M: This also works.

A: It does.

M: My parents, I think, found it amusing to name a baby girl after a male artist of such art-historical importance. That was their kind of humour, I suppose. Antonia is a lovely name, though. We're both named after men, as it turns out, though your name has been changed to the feminine. It was kind of your parents not to be so hell-bent on building character. [Laughter.]

And here you are: Antonia Green is a writer who is also working on the story of Irene Guernsey, and we met when I knocked on her door, which happens to be the home where Guernsey lived, and she graciously allowed me in. She is an accomplished writer who has written several books of award-winning poetry and three books of essays on the so-called ordinary beauty of the world, through the lens of art, photography, and landscape. And she might now be writing a novel, though it might be something else, I'm led to understand.

A: Yes, who knows what it is that I'm writing! Right now I'm just taking notes, lots and lots of notes. So. When we met, we felt in a way that we were working at cross-purposes. But the more we talked, it felt as though our two approaches could speak to each other, enlighten. We didn't want to shut anything out or down. For example, I don't so much want to tell a story as I want to accumulate facts, details, moods. I want to find the poetry around the person, Irene Guernsey, and to get at who she is through the very little that is known about her and her work.

M: And while I'm interested in these things, too, what I want to do is tell a visual story about her, a fictional re-imagining, which leads up to the theft, the photograph being stolen at the art gallery.

A: There's the fact that we don't know who stole the photograph. It's not important, but yet it's everything, don't you think?

M: It's this thing that I need to solve—or *resolve*, really, is a better way of looking at it. For the movie I want to make, I either need to find out who it is, or hint at who it might be, or just realize that not knowing who stole the photograph is at the core of the movie. Which is not really a traditional ending for a whodunnit.

A: And this is the kind of movie you want to make? A whodunnit?

M: [Laughs.] Well, actually, no. I guess I want to play with the idea of a mystery plot.

A: But what drew you to the story? Was it Irene's obscurity? Obviously, the art theft, the unsolved nature of it. But angels? What about angels?

M: That's what drew you, I think? Initially.

A: Okay, I'll confess, I've been interested in angels all my life.

M: You've seen them, then?

A: No!

M: Really?

A: Honestly, I haven't seen an angel. But I'm so interested in the stories of people who have, of people who really believe in them. Guardian angels, that sort of thing. For some people, angels are as real as you or me. But that aside, you're more interested in Irene herself. And I'm very interested in how you'll portray her in film. Because for me this is central. For one thing, she was not beautiful. She was an ordinary woman. She was plain, to be honest. Quite plain. I would like to see this honoured.

M: That doesn't happen often in Hollywood, or in any movie very often.

A: No, it doesn't. Everyone has to be larger than life, more beautiful. But she is larger than life, just in her own way.

M: Yes, I agree, even though so little is known about her, really. We have various conversations and reactions to her work. There isn't even a complete record of the photographs that she took or the ones she wanted to be part of her oeuvre. Did she think of her work in those terms at all, even? The other thing I want to think about is that photographs aren't usually stolen. If we go down the list of art thefts, photographs aren't especially prominent. Why steal something that could just be reproduced again? It makes me wonder what was special about this single photo. Where is the negative?

A: She doesn't have archives, as such. And much of her work is difficult to find. She showed her work in a couple of small gallery exhibits early on, but that's all.

A: I find it interesting how every now and then when I'm talking to you, it occurs to me, you're famous. And then I think about how angels are the opposite of that. They're anonymous, unseen. Society, I think, believes in movie stars. Does anyone believe in artists anymore, or did they ever? And some, *some*, believe in angels. But most people, they don't believe in angels. Do they? Maybe they do. Perhaps there are doubtful believers when it comes to angels. Half-believers or wishful believers.

M: And there are many different views on what an angel is or does.

A: Yes. Yes.

M: What do you think an angel is?

A: It's not that I haven't thought about that question a lot. A LOT. [Laughs.]

M: It's key, for me, to understanding Irene.

A: Did she believe, do you think?

M: And then we're talking about our belief in her belief. It's interesting, isn't it?

A: Oh yeah, it's like going in circles in a way. But I think she did believe. She saw. If you see, do you not believe?

M: I think you can fool yourself into not believing. Imagining that what you see is anything but what is there. Maybe she was just open to it, which is a kind of belief.

A: Open to the possibility of angels. And so they found her. Or did she create them? The illusion of them? Was she a photographer with tricks?

M: I don't think so. Experts who have examined her photos can't find the tricks. Could she have posed people in certain ways? I suppose. Most people assume this is the case.

A: It's not. She found angels, that's what I think. She saw the angels in people, maybe, or the ones that are always there and we just don't, as ordinary mortals, see. But you're not exactly an ordinary mortal, are you? Do you see them? As a famous movie star, do you see differently?

M: I don't see them at all. But I think they must be there. I have this feeling of being accompanied.

A: Accompanied. Yes. Yes.

[A long pause.]

M: And you? Living here, especially? You said you haven't seen an angel.

A: I'm waiting.

M: Ahh, okay. So tell me about when you moved here and how you found the place. Everything.

A: Okay, right, okay. Well, I had been working on a book about sorrow.

M: That sounds cheerful. [Laughter.]

A: I was interviewing and reading about people who lived with extreme sorrow and loss. How they can carry these terribly sad things inside them, but also function completely normally, and how most people who met them were unaware of this deeply, deeply sorrowful side of them. So it was as if they were constantly two different people, co-existing: the one who carried this unspeakable sorrow and pain, and at the same time, the one who was fine. Not just that they appeared to be fine, but they were fine. They had learned somehow to have their sorrow live in correspondence, in tandem, as though it were just beside them at another frequency. So they could experience joy, calm, happiness, too. One person described living with a personal sorrow as a magnetic force. So that she kept taking on more, and more kept being handed to her. She drew sorrow to her. It became immense. The weight was staggering. It made her heart beat differently, she said. She felt the world in a different way.

M: Actors often speak of something like this that they tap into for certain roles. Those who carry their own sorrow are quicker at it, more adept at tapping into that frequency, at putting their hands into the gloves of the apparition.

A: I asked this particular woman how she was able to attain this balance. And she said she'd never spoken about it until then, but that she'd always had this feeling of being accompanied. She laughed and talked about the library scene in the Wim Wenders movie, *Wings of Desire*. That's how it felt: someone there, but not there. Just feeling things along with you. And that was enough, enough to get through.

M: So this is what got you thinking about angels. How did you come upon Irene's work?

A: Like you, I heard about the art theft at the museum. It made the international news, as you know. I went to see the exhibit they'd created after the show. There was a woman

there, Sophie Angela Duras, who was conducting a sort of art project, a performance piece, in a way. She was influenced by the French artist Sophie Calle. Do you know her work?

M: Oh yes, of course, yes. And I studied the work Calle did after the Boston theft. I knew of her work before reading about the Edmonton theft.

A: So many people were affected by looking at the missing angel photograph, if one can look at something that isn't even there.

M: That's just it, isn't it?

A: These layers of a thing being looked at are meaningful. And the ways in which we understand how we see are telling.

M: Do we ever understand?

A: There's so much that we don't know or understand about how we see, how it affects us.

M: I sometimes wonder if I'm seeing things differently now, through this strange lens of so-called fame. Do I see any differently than when I was a kid or a young woman? Do I see differently because some people recognize me in the streets? Does that even make sense? I look at a bowl of fruit on the kitchen table, green pears, purple grapes, oranges, and I wonder if I see them differently now. But that can't be. They're still the same shapes and colours. I'm the same person. How does our vision change through time? How does our seeing evolve? Do we notice the way the light sways into the room and flits over the grapes, the dappling, the shadows, the way they seem at certain points of the day to be illuminated from within?

A: We experience things in the same way, don't we? But maybe we don't?

M: I want to believe that we do. But that at exactly the same time, we don't.

A: But let's consider that we aren't having the same experience. Because everything you've seen and done comes to bear on your current looking at a thing.

M: I had the same train of thought when I was looking at Irene's photos of the angel in the pheasant cage, that series.

Because I had a jolt of recognition. Not that I think I'm an angel, but one who feels trapped, scrutinized. Celebrity feels like being in a cage. In a way. People feel like they know you, which is the strangest thing. They piece together what you're like from small bits of information they're given. And perhaps it's the same for angels. We think we know what they're about. So I'm always going to be looking at the photographs through my lens of being an actor; that won't go away.

A: Let's also think about the way that being a movie star has people believing that you can save them. Not just the characters you play, but this idea that people have of *you*. They get obsessed. Possessive. Some of it can be sweet, but I imagine it can get frightening. They see something in you that you don't see. Is this accurate? We'd talked a bit about this before, off tape.

M: People want you to see them, to notice them. To magically see them, you know? To see and understand them with a shock of clarity. Maybe every human on earth wants that. As though that might save them. But you can only save yourself.

A: The shock of clarity. A kind of love. Which can happen, but when someone wants a famous person to see them like this, it's something else. It's not realistic. There are just too many people out there who are hoping you'll really "see" them, and the volume of souls makes it impossible.

M: Yes. I get that desire of the fan, though. I understand that wish for a shock of clarity moment, or love at first sight, or just some moment of true human understanding. It's not exactly reasonable, but it does happen. It can happen. One soul meeting another soul.

A: And yet, it's not a usual thing at all. I think it's an experience that belongs in ordinary life. I've met people who I think understood me right away. They really see me. We clicked, I guess you could say, though it was more than that. I mean, let's think about when we met. There was something there. I felt like I knew you. Though soon afterward, I thought

that was because you were famous. But it was more than just that. It's funny because I recognized you! But I didn't recognize you for being well-known. Not as the famous actor. Just as someone I thought I knew.

M: That's exactly it, and it was mutual, you know, which I think that feeling has to be. The current, the electricity, going both ways, the discovering that you're on the same frequency as another human.

A: And now this talking, this conversation. Which feels radical. It feels spacious.

M: I suppose that's why I'm interested in Irene. There was so much room around what she created. You could feel her subject matter gathering up strength to take off. In her photographs, there is that feeling of "It's the very moment before…"

A: The air is full and vibrating. There will be lift-off. The air will be dominated by the flight of her subject. Even in the caged angel series, one feels that the confinement is all a ruse. He could leave any time he likes; he could hit the air and be in the clouds so fast. The viewer somehow understands that implicitly. This is not a being who can be caged.

M: He is very damaged-looking in the beginning, and then as the series goes on, you can see he is opening up and coming into his powers. In the first photograph he has collapsed. He is fallen. Are they feathers even? The viewer can't be sure. If you only looked at this one photograph, a lot is unclear. Murky. One feels the photo was taken clandestinely. The figure looks down; the eyes might be open, they might be closed. It's not Rodin's *Thinker*. It's a figure we've not really seen before. My namesake's *Prisoners* comes to mind, I suppose.

A: It's okay to invoke your namesake.

M: It is, isn't it?

A: [Laughs.] Yes! And our angel does seem imprisoned, and I don't mean because he's in a cage. The imprisonment is inward. We can't fathom, it's not possible to know, it's

unknowable… what is he going through? This very unknow-ability is mysterious, and one feels it keenly. It's difficult to be in this state of not knowing with this picture. With this subject. It very much hurts to look at the first few photos. If there weren't the others…

M: Exactly. We get some relief.

A: It's not complete.

M: But it is some relief. The viewer, I, can go on looking because there is an improvement, a change.

A: Some of what hurts, for me, about looking at him in his really rough state is that if he's an angel, then he's not able to be that angel. So it's sort of a selfish interpretation. Who did he leave, what did he leave undone, what good works are now being left because he's caged and feeling poorly? I feel an urgency.

M: The photographs are powerful because they imme-diately engage our imaginations. We begin telling ourselves stories, trying to fill in the blanks. They're wonderful because they're mysterious. They don't give up everything. Or much of anything. My heart, though, it starts working when I look. I even feel it.

A: Yes, I know that feeling—it's not just a metaphorical thing. I feel it in my chest. My heart goes out to the old angel. I feel my heart trying to get out of my chest. And then the photos themselves all say to me, "Trust me," and I imme-diately respond, "I trust you." That's Irene, that part, isn't it?

M: Oh yes, yes, right. It's her.

A: Huh.

M: And so it's such a relief as he begins to move into health. You can sense his powers coming back on board. And it replicates this feeling so many of us have had, watching a loved one return from an illness, back into health. We relive that as we look through these photos. My aunt who had cancer—the treatments were awful. She kept her sense of humour for the most part, but there was an interval where it seemed she was just hanging on, and maybe she was letting

go at the same time. It was too much. Then there were small improvements, and then larger ones. It was excruciating, though. She could have left us at any time. She was making peace with her life. She was ready to go, even as she fought to stay. And all of this within a state of exhaustion so immense that she seemed to exist within a different time frame. A different realm altogether. She was swimming or floating, and her eyes were looking at us from the depths.

A: And most of us—we're both in our early 50s, aren't we? Yes. You're nodding. So by now, at this age, most people will have experienced a few deaths, leave-takings, endings. People we love have been taken from us. We've seen good deaths and not-so-good deaths.

M: Is that why it's so hard to forge new friendships? I mean, I don't find it easy to make friends.

A: Is it also your fame? Though, saying that, I feel like it's not easy at all, not at all, for me to make friends at this stage of my life. Which is another reason sitting here with you like this is so extraordinary to me.

M: I can't see that not everyone would want to be your friend!

[Laughter.]

A: Funnily enough, no. No, not everyone does want to be the friend of an odd woman with obscure interests and wild quirks and reclusive tendencies. I'm very set in my ways. And I don't care to change. Also, it is so very hard to get to know anyone well enough to really let them in. We don't all sit down and talk about a common interest for days. Which is maybe just a very good way to get to know someone.

M: It has been, hasn't it?

A: Yes, I think it really has been.

M: What happens when I leave? Is it strange to ask? I feel like a teenager. But do we remain friends after this? How do we stay in touch?

A: We do! I don't know how. Partly because you're the famous one. I'm just here, doing what I do. Writing. That

sort of thing. I don't want to impose on you. I don't want to make assumptions; I don't wish to presume.

M: But you feel friendship, a kinship?

A: Oh yes! Absolutely! Absolutely.

M: Oh, good, good. It will happen, I promise. Yes. Okay, so back to our angel. Should we talk about the theft? We've been leading up to it.

A: The photograph hasn't been recovered. There's some spotty security tape. It wasn't what you would call a *heist*. I mean, that implies that there was some planning and secrecy. We don't have Audrey Hepburn and Peter O'Toole hiding in a closet in the museum after hours. This thief just walked up to the work of art, took it off the wall, and walked out in broad daylight. The thief is most likely a woman, wearing winter clothes, and no one can figure out why the snow doesn't melt faster from her boots. I mean, that's the only clue, if you can call it a clue. It's weird.

M: *Weird* is a good word. It's interesting. It's a bit surreal, too, isn't it? Why did no one stop her? Did she look like she was supposed to be moving the work? She seemed purposeful. It's difficult to question purposeful actions.

A: And do you want to be this character? Or is it Irene that you want to play?

M: Well, both really. I want to be the one to get into who Irene really was, but I also want to understand the thief.

A: Can you do that?

M: Yes, I think so. I hope so.

A: Do you ever have any doubt about this project?

M: Doubt, for an artist, as you know, is always a part of the project. We can only fold it into the thing we're making. I wonder if anyone else will be as interested in Irene Guernsey as I am. But I'm so interested in her that I'm confident that I can convey that interest. That's not where the doubt lies, I don't suppose. I'm okay with relying on my belief that one's interest, the interest itself, can carry a project.

A: Living here, I feel as though I'm a bit closer to Irene. That's probably a mistaken feeling. But I wander around the property, through the trees that she walked through, and on the paths she walked upon, and into the various pheasant coops, the old angel's coop, and there's a presence. I can imagine her better. Still, it doesn't make sense to need to be here.

M: You were drawn.

A: It was just a small pilgrimage, at first. I came to see where she lived, as others would seek out the home of Georgia O'Keefe. But the place was for sale, and I had inherited some money at the same time. I took it as a sign.

M: I would have, too.

A: I don't know if I'll live here forever, but at least until I finish my book. The thing is, I feel things out here I've never felt. And that's where *my* doubt lies: how can I make that part of what I'm writing about Irene? Does it matter? I think it's important. And yet.

M: What are these things that you're feeling? Can you put it into words?

A: Most people would think me mad, but you're an actor, so I can talk about my feelings.

[Laughter.]

A: Okay. Well, we talked earlier about feeling accompanied. And as I walk down the path through the pheasant pens, the ones that lead into the forest, down to the lake, I can imagine Irene so clearly. It's not some supernatural thing, it's very real. It would make for bad TV. I don't feel as though it's magical. It feels normal, ordinary. It's an everyday thing. I'm used to it, even.

M: How will you approach this in your writing?

A: I like this question. Because though we have much in common with our projects, my goal is to make a book that could never be made into a film. I love films, but I also love the idea that a book is a thing unto itself, that it is something potentially so unique and strange that it could only be itself.

Of course, I'm writing about photographs, which can really only be what they are. I don't know how I'm going to accomplish this, but that's the goal. I could see writing a book that just describes the photographs as clearly as possible.

M: Books get made into films, but rarely do films get turned into books. Not really. There are books about films, but films aren't thought of as translatable in that way.

A: I suppose they could be, but is it a market thing? Maybe.

M: Right.

A: Thinking about it makes me want to attempt to turn a movie into a novel. It would be a strange novel, though. A cross between an interpretation and a translation and an ekphrastic utterance.

M: Maybe what I'm most interested in is how Irene Guernsey seems to translate humans into angels. That kind of translation. From seeing good, to photographing the ethereal. It's not a clear equation. But translation never is.

A: Can we talk about what it is to be ordinary? I think when we're talking about the presence of angels and movie stars, it's helpful to think about ordinary humans, too.

M: I think about what it is to be ordinary. I feel that I'm ordinary.

A: You're not.

[Laughter.]

M: I was once, though. We're laughing, but I do know what you mean. I'll never be thought of in that way by most, again. Even if I quit acting and moved to some remote place, people would know or find out. It's part of who I am, being on the big screen. It's in my DNA by now. I'm seen differently, and to be frank, I see myself differently. In one way, though, I still feel at my core that I'm myself, me. Ordinary me. And yet simultaneously, there's that part of me that feels and even knows very deeply that I'm well, Someone. I'm special. I have a talent. Which sounds very narcissistic. I feel less that I'm important, but I believe that

the work I do has some importance. The work gives me a type of confidence. I'm not necessarily a confident person in all things, but when it comes to the work, yes. I have an ego. I think I'm generally a humble person who sometimes tricks herself into feeling powerful and creative and godlike.

A: No, I get it. You need to feel that way to do what you do.

M: But there are ordinary moments, if we want to call them that. Is anyone really ever ordinary? Also, one starts to wonder if it's all acting. Playing a role. When one is back to one's so-called ordinary life, is one then playing at "ordinary?" I sound like an ass right now, don't I? We'll have to delete this!

A: No! You don't! Not at all. This is a place to work things through. To think aloud. I mean, I consider myself a completely ordinary person. I'm using the word *ordinary* to mean that I'm not famous or capable of performing incredible feats of athleticism or art or science. No one knows who I am. But I'm not suggesting that I'm not a wonderful human being, you know? I have that much confidence!

M: You're a writer. This is not ordinary.

A: Well, I'm not known. Let's say that. And that's fine. Honestly. It's good, really. I just want to work, and be left alone, out here on this piece of land near the lake.

M: It's a fine thing. To be here.

A: Shall we take a break? Would you like a glass of wine?

M: Where did we leave off?

A: I don't know, but I've been thinking that this is as much about two women speaking from the same dimension as it is anything else. And I've been thinking about the way that you can only say certain things in certain conversations. The way that one might say something that they hadn't thought about before. But then it becomes clear. And changes the way one moves forward, or sees oneself, others, the world. Which is why we need to keep

talking and make spaces for conversations. I've also been thinking about the difference between us. Me, an ordinary mortal who hasn't had her hair cut professionally for over a decade. I've never had my nails done. I've heard of eye-lash weaving, but I don't know what it is. I can't wear false things—eyelashes, nails, you know. And then you, well, you're so perfect.

M: I'm manicured. I'm a doll. Well, I do let most of that go when I'm not working. It's already wearing off. Soon my nails will be rubbish, I promise you.

A: Part of the reason I came here, to live out here by the lake, near Irene, or the ghost of her, is to let myself be me, for once. How many women get to do that? Some would use the word *wild,* but that's not it. I just want to be myself with-out any pressures. I want to be free to write things without coming to any point. I want to write as a bird might fly, in a direction of my choosing, free of obstacles. My flying is in multiple directions at once. Here it is lithe and balletic, there it is intense and furious, and then again it is dreamy, then fiery, then confidently muscular and airy and sexy. At last it is so quiet and faint it is a wisp.

M: What if we were left to be creative in the ways that we needed to be without recourse to a readership or viewership? Of course I want an audience, but the audience would catch up to me. I'm ahead of the audience, doubling back. That sounds pretentious, but there's something there to explore. I think Irene was ahead of us, she knew something. She had enough money that she didn't have to care. It's always the money, isn't it? Still.

A: Oh, yes, very often. An invisible support that lets the work happen. An inheritance, a rich partner, at least rela-tively speaking. An abundance of grants. Some kind of sti-pend or legacy or trust fund. In my case, a small inheritance. It won't last forever, but I'm being foolish and using it now while my creative juices are flowing.

M: Do you think they stop flowing?

A: Oh, the accepted version of this is that anyone can create at any time. Of course. But it changes if you don't attend to it, is my theory. The genius of creativity shouldn't be put off. It's deep, and to get to the depths is a life's work. Some people can get there later, but I'm not taking that chance.

M: There are moments in an artist's life when one is filled with an unearthly confidence without which the work would not be made. I think of that time as an angel, if a period of time could be called such.

A: I agree.

M: What a tangent. Which is the point of these conversations. That we can talk about whatever comes up.

[Short interval of silence.]

A: Yes, but, okay. Let's get back to the photographs. The early ones, where the viewer must squint to see what's happening. You move backwards and forwards before the photo. Your brain fills in various shapes until you're seeing an angel. But are you? They're in black and white, they're grainy, moody, ethereal. From up close it seems like you're looking at a boy or a girl, but if you move back, and sometimes to the side, an angel appears. And then once you've seen it, it's there. Indelible.

M: So the angel can be explained away, as though Irene has seen what's happening in the background, in the natural surroundings, and simply waited until all the elements lined up a certain way with the subject of the photo. Isn't that quite miraculous, too? This kind of art—the art of waiting.

A: I completely agree! And I do think that's what's happening. But at the same time I feel as though something else is happening simultaneously. She does in fact see an angel. We do in fact witness the coming into being of an angel. The seeing is, in a way, the becoming. One is *angelled*.

M: This is certainly what the experience of looking at her photos is, as well. At first, I just looked at the subject. There is an aura, an innocence, a real beauty in the way this

ordinary boy or girl or young adult is portrayed, captured. I think *captured* is the correct word.

A: Innocence. It's a rare thing in this world. It's difficult to even put in words because it's not something that's talked about.

M: Innocence is a realm that is so far from our everyday life.

A: Was the thief innocent?

M: We'd have to rethink innocence.

A: Does it have to do with motive? I don't read crime fiction. I don't usually think about crimes. Was it a crime? Technically, yes. But why would she have taken it?

M: Do you think this is solvable?

A: No, honestly, no.

M: I think that this is okay. Not knowing. Leaving that open. The truth is often like that. The truth here is a stroke of the pen, the open gesture of a hand, an "I don't know."

A: And there are different approaches to writing or filming this. One can offer possibilities. One can leave it open, as is. One can imagine one ending. One can pretend one knows, or lead the viewer forward with what seem to be incontrovertible facts. One may suggest. One may haunt.

M: One may haunt. Or be haunted.

A: We are definitely haunted.

M: I don't want to interpret. That, I do know. I want to show and entice.

A: Some days I think I just want to talk about it. The theft. I want to just talk about Irene. What does she mean? How does she signify for us, right here, now? What does it mean to sit here and talk about her and her art?

M: It feels a bit radical. A bit private, in the way that women talk about things.

A: When we sit down, I never know what I'll say. What we'll talk about.

M: Yesterday, I'll say for the tape, we went for a walk together. It was a bit foggy and brisk, frost on the edges of

the flowers. A lovely late fall day. The sun shining on the frost when we started out. And then by the time we had wended our way back, it had burned off.

A: And what were we talking about. It was so intense. Can you remember?

M: As I was describing the walk just now, I was thinking about all the emotions I felt. But what did we talk about? Well, we were thinking about Irene and how we were walking where she did, and we imagined her with her camera around her neck. We walked into the trees a little. The undergrowth is very thick right now. As though no one, no thing, has been in the woods much of late. The paths are visible, but there are branches across. They're not easy to traverse. It's all closing over. Like Irene's story, I suppose, a bit. It's there, but it's difficult to access. And some of it is not particularly navigable. At a certain point we just backed out, turned around. Tried another way. Another path or point of access. We still got where we wanted to go.

A: It seems rather symbolic, now.

M: Do you think Irene felt ordinary? Do you know what I mean?

A: I do, and I was wondering the same thing as we were peering through the trees, trying to see angels. There was that point where we decided you would go ahead and walk into the thicket, sort of will yourself into a thicker part of the trees. And I looked from farther off. But it was you, and I couldn't make angel wings appear, however I squinted or moved. Maybe it was a silly thing to try. I had wondered if she willed the wings into being, or if by looking deeply they somehow had appeared—shadows and branches and leaves and the light aligning. Either way I think Irene had this gift.

M: But did she understand that? Did she think it was a special skill? Or was she unnerved by her ability to see?

A: Did she just accept it?

M: I would like to believe that.

A: The belief that a woman could accept her gifts, her talent, and just create.

M: Without doubt. Without self-censure. Without any remorse. Just a pure exploration through her art of the world around her.

A: It doesn't sound radical.

M: We're back. I realize we haven't said when we've stopped and started. I imagine if we play these recordings back, it's going to seem one long stream of consciousness.

A: Well, it's just for us, really, anyway. I promise I won't try to sell them on the Internet or to some gossip magazine.

M: I hate to tell you, but I don't think they'd buy them.

[Laughter.]

A: That's okay. But should we try to be more systematic? What questions should we try to answer here? Because soon you'll be leaving.

M: Yes, we talked about that while we were doing the dishes this morning. Good scones, by the way. Very nice jam. We treated ourselves, didn't we? And the coffee… it was wonderful. Thank you for that.

A: It was lovely to share that with you.

M: So, what questions have we left? Well, many of them. Does it matter that we don't know why the photograph was stolen, or how exactly she made it out of the building without being noticed? And who she is? Was she connected to Irene? Why Irene's photo and not one of the other artworks? Who is Irene, really? What do we really know about Irene?

A: And what about angels? What are our questions around angels?

M: The whole thing is a nest of questions, really.

A: Exactly. We can ask questions upon questions. There are no answers, only speculation. It's all speculation.

M: Such a good word, *speculation*.

A: Which—I'm looking it up—means to theorise or conjecture, but comes from the sixteenth-century Latin, "observe from a vantage point," "to look." And it's derived from *specula*, a word meaning "watchtower."

M: Which is what Irene did, she watched from a vantage point—away from, I suppose.

A: How will you make your film about a woman watching and waiting? And then about a theft that no one can solve? Is it enough?

M: I'm beginning to think my film is also about us. Would you like to be in my film?

A: Oh, no, you don't!

[Laughter.]

M: But why not?

A: Because. Because...... because I am just an ordinary person trying to write a book. I like being invisible. I don't want to be seen, even a rendition of me, on the big screen.

M: Well, I never presume my films will make it that far. I don't. It's not healthy.

A: But I know that a film by you has a very good chance of making it. I've Googled you! I know!

M: It was better when you had no idea who I was.

A: Better for whom?

M: Well, me, of course.

[Laughter.]

M: But seriously, why can there not be a film about just two women talking? One that's not a documentary, I mean.

A: It wouldn't seem truthful, maybe. A conversation is meant to be real. And a fictional conversation, a long one, how could that seem real? Could it?

M: But if it seems real, that's enough. That would be enough.

A: A fictional conversation, though, would mean the author is having a conversation with herself. The actors, then. They would have to speak the lines as though they were coming up with them, just then.

M: That's the actor's job.

A: But would it seem real? The viewer would be suspending their disbelief in all the usual ways, I suppose. The problem would be time. A conversation occupies too much of it,

is too linear, or too meandering. And a person in a conversation is engaged in a way that an eavesdropper cannot be.

M: I'm not sure about the eavesdropper. I love eavesdropping. Also, what does it mean when two women get together to talk? What is the role of the audience? How can we ask more of them? Is that fair or possible? I mean, it's not, it's not.

A: And what does it mean when we get together to talk about making things like films and books about other women? Which reminds me, we need to talk about the thief. A woman thief.

M: Why do you think she stole the photograph?

A: It was personal for her. She was attached to the photograph in some way. Was it her in the photo?

M: Was she the angel seen through the falling snow, the one standing on the hill in the snow?

A: It's a possibility. I mean, part of what we're doing here is imagining all the possibilities. One of the possibilities in all this is that we both leave the question alone.

M: Right, yes, yes. I have also thought that one of the possibilities in all this is that we both leave here, this house, and neither of us end up writing about Irene or making a film about her, or the angels. We leave that wondering here, in this house. It is a possibility.

A: What's another possibility, though?

M: I've considered putting an ad in the paper, on the Internet. You know, *thief wanted*. I've considered what it would be like if she, too, were in this room.

A: And if she were?

M: Are you the thief?

A: Let's imagine that I'm the thief.

M: Let's.

A: I'm the thief.

M: That's a profound act, a statement. It's an annunciation. Because now I have to readjust my beliefs. Yes, it's an annunciation.

A: Let me say it again. I'm the thief.

M: Truly?

A: Yes.

A: I sometimes think if we could understand what it is to be a star, we would also understand more about angels.

M: Really?

A: Let me think through the connections aloud. The thing is, fans need stars, but stars also need fans in order to be stars. And the same is true for angels. If we didn't believe in them, would they be what they are? So let's think about stars for a moment. I wonder also what happens to you as a star when you say to yourself, yes, I'm a "star." The word *star*, even, when did that start being used to refer to anything other than celestial bodies? It started with Chaucer and Shakespeare and was used in the eighteenth century and again when British actors were attempting to remake themselves in the U.S. when their careers had fizzled out in the 1820s. Of course, when the big screen came into being, so did the concept of star quality and the cult of the star. The fans are the mortals, always, and the stars are the gods, and it's the transcendence and the communion between the mortals and gods that is at the core of the angel-human connection.

M: You've done some research!

A: I have. I'm a nerd that way. My question is, what happens when an ordinary human realizes they're a star? And what about angels? Do they know they're angels?

M: Oh, okay, okay.

A: Do you think of yourself as a star? I mean you are, obviously, a star. So when did that transformation happen? When did you go, *oh, I'm a star now*? Did someone else confer this upon you, or…

M: [Laughs.] Well. I'll be serious. I wanted to be an actor and the star thing just happened. My goal had not been to be "a star," because that is a ridiculous thing to want to be. I wanted to act, to be in the process of acting. I wanted to

work. I guess there are some people who want that star thing, that attention, but not me. So then it happened.

A: It did! Were you surprised?

M: Listen, the first time you end up on a red carpet, you feel like a fraud, and it's all acting there, too. And this idea of having fans. Wow. Some of them are truly fanatic. It's surprising. I don't know where that super fandom comes from, though parts of it are nice. You feel reassured by them, I guess. But it's also surreal. I'm not knocking fans at all. They're very often engaging people. Maybe the fans are the angels.

A: You interact with them?

M: Not very much, though once in a while. I want to stay real. I don't want them to think I believe in that mortal and god set-up, you know, that you mentioned earlier. That doesn't work for me.

A: But do you see it around you?

M: Okay, yes, but I don't pay much attention to how others navigate that realm. I should, I suppose. I just want to work. Of course, you're foolish if you don't attempt to understand the way things are. That goes for any kind of existence, though, I think? Would you agree?

A: Sort of like office politics, you mean? Understanding the lay of the land.

M: Right.

A: Does being a star correlate in any way with being an angel? I mean, maybe an angel just wants to do the work, be the angel, and not be all angelic or feel so removed. Maybe they'd just like to go out for a burger without being recognized and asked for autographs.

[Laughter.]

A: Okay, so I'm interested in what it does to an actor to play an angel? What does an actor bring to the role of an angel?

M: There have been lots of movie angels.

A: Yes.

M: But this movie will only have angels peripherally, the ones in the photographs, likely.

A: Who will play Irene? You?

M: Yes, I think I have to. I want to.

A: Maybe Irene is an angel.

M: I know. I've thought about this. I don't know. I'm not really certain.

A: Okay, so let's go back to belief. Do we believe in stars in the same way we believe in angels? When did we start believing in angels? And do we still believe in them?

M: Some people do believe in them. Many.

A: But more people believe in stars. Rock stars, movie stars, reality TV stars, even sports stars.

M: Fame is so fleeting, so intangible. The work is what matters.

A: Yes, yes.

M: Angels are messengers, the word comes from their role as messengers. And I do often feel as though people want me to tell them something. To be changed by what I tell them. Not always, but this feeling arises. They want meeting me to have some kind of meaning. I don't know if it can, or if it does. That part is out of my hands, really.

A: Does it bother you that people want this thing from you, that's so totally outside of what you do, which is to act and create films?

M: Well, it's interesting, I think. I'm curious about people, so no, it doesn't bother me. If I have any power to make someone feel better about their life, or their existence, I take that as a gift. I'm not going to dismiss them.

A: What do you have in common with Irene?

M: Mystery.

A: Ahhhh.

M: I hadn't thought about that.

A: The word arrives.

M: But yes, I think it's the correct word. Mystery. The need to live with mystery. To not so much seek it, but make

it present. It's there always, I think. The question of how to manifest mystery. That is my question, one that I live with.

A: Is Irene's life, then, a vehicle, to sit with this question, to share it?

M: Oh yes, I think that's part of it.

A: She didn't necessarily know what was happening when she began taking her photos, but she was open to what appeared, what she captured. She followed it.

M: We're imagining things, speculating, but that's what I think happened for her. I've just had this thought that what we're doing here—the questioning, the sitting with the questions—this is actually what an angel is. This force, this act, what we're doing, enacting, is a feather held up by the air itself.

A: There's a feather in the air between us, and with our breath it's held by our conversation. Hovering at a midpoint, sometimes moving closer to you or to me.

M: And this is what an angel is.

A: In the Talmud, angels are said to be fire. And in Islamic belief, an angel is light. This is meant metaphorically. The angel is a part of the unseen, immaterial world. It has been said that perhaps each angel exists at a "specific temperature" or a "specific wavelength" of light. One controversial philosopher, Origen, in the third century, believed that "every soul was given a choice, and those who chose well became angels, and those who chose less well became human, and those who made bad choices became demons."

M: To sit down and think through that in the third century. That's pretty amazing.

A: I like thinking of angels as a specific wavelength of light. Or as fire!

M: When did angels start having wings?

A: Okay, now you're testing me. I think I read that they first started to be depicted in art with wings in the 4th century, and scholars say this was because of the influence of images of Nike and Eros. There is a Muslim tradition that describes the archangels, Gabriel and Michael, as having 600 wings.

But in general, historians agree that our modern idea of the angel, halo and wings, comes from the 5ᵗʰ century. There are scenes in the Roman Church of Santa Maria Maggiore in the 5ᵗʰ century that depict angels in the way that we recognize angels today.

M: We've never really talked about the halos. Irene's images are of angels with wings, but there aren't any halos, are there?

A: Let's see, let's think. Okay. No, I can't remember seeing any halos in her photographs.

[A pause.]

M: So can we talk about The Angel, the one in the cage, Irene's angel? That series of photos.

A: Is that what we've been leading up to? I think so. Those photos tell a story.

M: They haunt me.

A: We've put them into an order. They were never in any book or show. Not these ones. Shall I say how I found them? Okay. They were in the pheasant pen, the golden one, near the house, when I moved here. Hidden, a little hidden. In a dry box, up in the rafters, wrapped in plastic. It's a sturdy pen, good roof. But still, I'm amazed that they're in good condition.

M: He arrives and there are photos of him sleeping. Is he sleeping? Maybe he's sleeping. And then, he's ill, he's quite dirty, dusty. She's captured the caked-on mud, the dustiness. It's extraordinary.

A: There are photographs of line-ups. People waiting. There is a man on a stool before the cage, holding a book, and he seems to be reading out loud. Others wait. In some there are 5 or 6 people standing in front of the pheasant pen. You can see through them; there he is lying on the bed. There is a figure on a bed. My eyes see wings, but anyone else might see a strange garb, blankets, a lump on a bed, reclining.

M: I keep thinking, how could I capture all this, turn her photos, and her taking the photos, into a film? He arrives and is hurt, damaged. Then later we see him walking around,

flexing his wings. And later still his wings start to bloom. There is suddenly colour. In the spring, his wings are like leaves, miraculously unfurling into the sparkling champagne light. There is one where he is squatting down on a hill in the golden hour; his wings are now powerful, both of them. He looks as though he is going to erupt into the sky.

A: He could, but he doesn't quite yet. It's as though he's waiting for something.

M: That's another question, isn't it? What's he waiting for? He could leave, he could fly.

A: Could he? It does feel like anything could happen. There is so much tension captured in the photo. The air is vibrating. Does it feel that way to you too?

M: Oh yes, and because of that, I can't help asking myself, *what is the story?* How can any of this be captured, transformed into a film?

A: We have the photos.

M: It seems sacrilege to try to recreate any of it cinematically. But otherwise, how will anyone know about the art that Irene created? I don't want her to disappear.

A: Part of me wants to just keep her to myself. But if we don't talk about women artists, if we don't keep them in the air with our breath, they'll vanish.

M: She deserves to be more widely known. And not just for the theft of her photograph from the art gallery. Are we not responsible, also, for this? For her?

A: It's a place to start from. Women are experts in passing along messages in this way. Sharing what we know. There are other channels than the obvious ones.

M: Irene was receptive. Her camera allowed in the light. The light of angels. The art of photography, it occurs to me, is so perfect for depicting angels, since angels are light, and the camera is an instrument of capturing light.

A: But we will never know anything about her, there is so little written about her. Are there photographs of Irene? I've not seen any. She was the woman behind the camera. There are no diaries. Was she not made of light,

too? Is she not an instrument of light? Are we? You are an instrument of light.

M: There are the transcribed interviews. We no longer even have the cassettes they were based upon.

A: It's a miracle that we have those, even. Xaviere's interviews, found in a secondhand store on Whyte Avenue. There is one photo of Irene, remember. Yes.

M: There is another part of the story that I think we're forgetting to talk about. So, the photograph was stolen, and then there was a woman who suggested the art gallery put up an empty frame to sort of commemorate the theft. And then people started coming to see the show because of that. She recorded their impressions. And there are a lot of photos out there where people posed in front of the blank frame—it was a big gold thing, with just black paper under glass. When they photographed themselves, there were often other reflections that appeared in the glass. Shapes, forms. Interesting things are happening in those reflections. It was when Instagram was just starting to be a thing. Selfies.

A: Yes, and then she interviewed people about how the loss of the photograph affected them. And she published a book called *Everything Affects Everyone*. Her name is Sophie Angela Duras.

M: Have you met her? Could we bring her here? Into our conversation?

A: Yes… I know her. I've met her, though only briefly. Let me see if I can find her before you leave. So, you're on Instagram?

M: Well, one has to be these days, I suppose. I am. I'm not terribly good at it.

A: You don't have someone doing it for you?

M: Some do, but the best ones are real. You have to do it yourself, for that to happen.

A: I think Sophie Angela is on Instagram, and you can see that she has collected photos of that time. I guess people have sent them to her, and she's assembled them. Shall we look at them together? We can look on my phone, and keep

recording with yours? Isn't technology wonderful? Well, it's horrible, but it's also wonderful.

[Laughter, sounds, rustling.]

A: Here are some of her photos of people standing in front of the empty gilded frame. Hashtag StolenAngel. And maybe it's significant to mention that the photograph has been replaced with a black surface rather than white. That was also a choice. Symbolically obvious, I suppose, but why not white? Something translucent?

M: Right, all these choices, in art, are meaningful. So, there are hundreds of people posing in front of an empty gilded frame. Some have their backs to the camera, others are selfies, and others have been taken perhaps by a bystander or friend, taken from further away. They show more of the room.

A: That there are all these people somewhat self-consciously taking photos of themselves with an empty frame—they're picturing themselves in the place of an angel. It's a novelty for them. A bit of a joke. But some of the people look serious. Look at this one, very grave.

M: Yes, that's a very serious look.

A: And then others are trying to look beatific, it seems.

M: Or the opposite, rather devilish. There are some that are trying to do it surreptitiously. They just want to quickly sneak in a selfie. And then others are just right into it, posing, confident. It's the fame of the missing photograph, the theft, that interests, rather than the photograph itself. They want to catch a little of that notoriety. Or maybe they want to be a part of that history.

A: This sharing of her work, though, let Irene become a little more known. The theft elevated her work, or drew attention to it. She'd been unknown, really, in spite of being in a show. No one had much heard of her. She had no name recognition. After the show she would have been forgotten, mainly. Yes, there were likely some who would remember her work. But she wasn't being written about. She wasn't in the newspapers or on the Internet. If you Googled her, you'd have found very little. But then after the theft, her name

was everywhere. She, her art, was gaining traction in the art world. Even if it was thanks to #StolenAngel.

M: Though I doubt this would have been a goal for her while she was living…

A: I think she wanted to be more known, but wasn't willing to play games or promote herself in the ways that the establishment required. It took away from the work, or took her away from her work, more accurately.

M: We'd like to believe that great art is like cream rising to the top. But so much gets lost. Or buried or forgotten.

A: What is the artist's responsibility to the art? And what to the public? If you've made something, to what extent is it incumbent upon you to get it out there into the world?

M: More and more that responsibility is placed on the artist.

A: The art, for Irene maybe, was secondary to her experience with angels. Or, her art was a means, a way of processing what she saw.

M: Maybe that's what art is, though: an experience with angels. Or an experience with the divine. That communion was enough.

A: She was content to be outside the market because she had enough money to live. She wanted to make art. And she did.

M: The art she made didn't rely on a market to exist.

A: Filmmaking is tied to the market. It would be quite difficult to make a film and not care if anyone wanted to watch it.

M: There are too many people involved. The actor is the least of it, in many ways.

A: But you're communing with the divine. What is film if not a medium of light?

M: That's the pull, the hope, and there are moments. If you didn't have them…

A: Is this what draws you to Irene?

M: When I saw her work there was a spark for me. I can't really explain why, but there was a pull toward it, inexorable. I didn't question it. There are some things that, artistically, it's pointless to question. Rather, I accepted.

Michelangelo and Antonia and Sophie Angela

A: We're talking again about Irene Guernsey and the theft of her photograph at the Art Gallery of Alberta several years ago. I just wanted to say at the beginning of our recording, that I talked to Sophie Angela Duras and enticed her to come and meet you, Michelangelo, and she's here right now and joining our conversation.

M: The truth is we've been talking for a while, the three of us, and only thought to bring out the recording device just now.

[Laughter.]

A: So welcome, Sophie Angela. I think you said you prefer Sophie Angela to just Sophie.

S: Yes, does that sound pretentious? I don't always push for it, but this is what my parents have called me all my life, and I feel more like *me* with both names.

A: Lovely. And no, it's not at all pretentious.

M: Michelangelo is pretentious.

[Laughter.]

A: So I lured you out here, telling you that a filmmaker was here who was making notes and gathering impressions

for the movie she intends to make about Irene Guernsey. And that was enough to draw you here.

S: Oh, certainly, and in reality, I've wanted to see the house where Irene lived for some time, so that alone was enough to bring me here.

A: And then you arrive and you meet Michelangelo, and of course you know who she is immediately. Unlike me.

S: Well, I was gobsmacked, as they say.

[Laughter.]

S: I still can't quite believe I'm in her presence. Is this really happening? I didn't think I was the type to be star-struck but it turns out I am. It's a bit embarrassing.

M: But we're going to talk about Irene, and I promise you, you won't think much of me for long.

S: Oh, I will!

[Laughter.]

A: So we've been talking for a while, you've been here for a few hours, and we've looked over the pheasant pen, had a tour of where our decrepit old angel lived. We're all feeling a bit possessive of him now. And we've seen the hill he took off from, where Irene took those photos. And we've looked through, together, some of Irene's well-known photos. And we even touched upon the work that you did at the gallery where the photo was stolen.

S: I'm really hoping to be in the movie, now!

[Laughter.]

S: But okay, it's really interesting, because I'm still, years later, receiving notes from the people I talked to at the gallery. And they're talking about how that exhibition, and the art theft, changed their lives. Not always in huge ways, but in subtle ways, small ways. It expanded things for them. The way they looked at their place in the world.

M: Was it the fact of the theft? Or was it more because of...

S: The theft brought them there. But the theft changed things for them, no doubt about it. And then for me.

M: Your life changed because of the theft.

S: And the people. Their stories. That theft, and all the thefts that art consists of. We know that cliché, *all art is theft,*

but when a work of art is stolen, we're plunged into that reality. The art theft became in my mind a work of art unto itself. I felt almost as though I were creating a conceptual work of art about a performance art piece—the theft itself—which was interacting with the art of a photographer. It was a weird arrangement, you know? And I think that someone might look at that and think it was a bit rarefied, a bit esoteric. But for me there was this authentic thread that took anyone who was interested through that labyrinth.

A: Now you have me thinking about Icarus!

M: Let's come back to Icarus. And Ariadne. All that.

A: Yes, let's not forget.

M: This is the project that you were working on really, regarding the theft. Tell me how you began, what you were trying to accomplish. Let's start at the beginning.

S: I was in the gallery already. I was feeling my way.

M: You had in mind that you would just observe and write things down.

S: And maybe I would overhear things. But I didn't know how possible any of it would be. I just wanted to be in the space and let things happen. I wasn't really all that hopeful. I didn't know how far the sound would carry; I didn't know how obtrusive my presence might be. People might talk more quietly because I was in the room. Or they might regulate their gestures more. I had no way of knowing how my presence would affect anything.

A: One more variable.

S: I wanted to see how being there would change me. My project seems quite outward, but there was also this aspect of it that was inward. The unstated part of the project.

A: It's going to be that way, isn't it? We make art to discover one thing, explore one avenue or thread, but we're the ones who are changed. We're called to something and we don't even know exactly why, but we know somehow it will affect us. I pity those who can't or don't go where and when they are called.

S: Exactly!

A: I find myself being changed already, as I research and write notes for my book. And Michelangelo. You must feel this?

M: I do. I do.

[Pause.]

M: What I'm curious about—I'm curious as to whether you saw the person who stole the photograph? Where were you? Well, you were probably asked these types of questions when the theft was investigated?

S: Interestingly, not really. I wasn't much of a suspect or a witness for that matter. I was disappointed, really. I mean, I thought it could end up being part of my project, the questioning by the police. But they could see where I was on the security tape. I'd gone for lunch. The gallery was so empty at that time. It was a cold day, the show hadn't gotten the press that it would get after the theft, and I'd been asking myself if what I had in mind would work. I'd not thought it would go on as it did go on. The theft changed everything.

M: When you came back from lunch, what was it like?

S: Oh, chaos! Chaos. But also a sort of excitement. They shut the space down, of course. I mean, immediately everyone knew that this would bring attention to the show and to the gallery. There was fear—what if it had been found that the gallery had neglected some part of security? What if trust in the system would be eroded? But then, the idea was to bring attention to the art, the artist, and to, well, mainly to the gallery.

M: And attention really was garnered.

S: There was a lot of surprise at how far-reaching it was, thanks to social media.

M: This is how I first heard about the theft, about Irene, and her photographs. And it really got me thinking about how all art relies on other art. I wanted to make art about her art. I wanted the conversation around that to be art.

A: You wanted to be the angel of her art, you wanted to watch over it, send it out as a message…

M: You too?

A: I sort of feel as though this is what all art is, just finding a way to say things through other things. In this case, angels. But when I say *angels*...

M: It could be about anything, but the message is...

A: The message is...

S: We don't always know what the message is until after it's been sent, maybe long after it's been sent. After it's arrived, we don't even know then, always. It takes time. There are different ways of knowing. Of understanding. It doesn't always need to be deciphered, just received.

M: It needs to be sent!

A: Amen. The message needs to be sent.

M: Maybe that's actually the message. Send the message. Keep sending messages.

S: On all frequencies.

M and A: Yes!

S: Does it matter how Irene came to photograph the angels? Have you ever wondered if it was all a set-up? Models hired, that sort of thing. Because when I make my art pieces, I don't always wait for the art to come to me. I will it into being. I arrange for it to happen. I hire actors if I need to.

M: Do you sense that was what she did?

S: No. I really don't. It seems real. I just completely suspend my disbelief when I look at her work. I just believe in what I see, what she's shown me. Not so different than if I were looking at a Chagall angel or one by an Italian Renaissance artist.

M: Let's return to the idea of the castoff feathers. Icarus.

A: Let's talk about Ovid's version. Daedalus, the father, collects feathers from birds as they fly above. They're trapped in the labyrinth, father and son are, so part of his art is a waiting game. And then, when Daedalus has enough, he melts wax, he constructs wings so that his son Icarus can escape. But of course, Icarus flies too close to the sun. Would you

like me to read from the translation? Okay, "The wax melted. Icarus moved his bare arms up and down, but without their feathers they had no purchase on the air. Even as his lips were crying his father's name, they were swallowed up in the deep blue waters which are called after him."

M: Right, right. I can't help but notice that the words *father* and *feather* are one letter off.

[Pause.]

M: So let's turn to the words of one of my favourite writers, Hélène Cixous. Who says, "There is no artist without castoff feathers."

We have all been grafted, we artists, with these feathers. We pick up where the other has left off. We wild hearts, we are all borrowing, stealing, flying. One folds into the other; we lift, we rise, the feathers drop again, spiraling through the air, aloft and then spinning down and down. We hold out our hands, those of us looking skyward, and we hope and we wander, hands out cupped, ready; we catch. Feathers float right into our hands. We wait, we watch. We capture. And away we go again. Skyward, always into the blue. Every single time we are in awe, it's a surprise, we didn't know we could fly.

A: As we're talking, I just keep writing down questions.

M: Can you read them out?

A: Okay, yes. Really? Okay. Yes. Here:

Why do angels appear, do you think?

Why do artists appear?

Why do we ignore artists?

Why do angels not always recognize each other? Or do they?

Why don't all the angels fly? And why don't we see murmurations of angels in the sky? What aren't we seeing that's right in front of us?

Who are angels? Who? Or how? Or what?

Why do we need angels? Do angels need us?

How do angels change things? How do they affect us?

If angels are messengers, what are the messages?

Are angels constructed? Do they appear fully formed? Do they happen?

Who invented angels?

Do angels invent other angels?

What are the responsibilities of angels?

[Pause.]

M: We've been sitting with the questions.

A: Are they strange, do you think? Is it strange to just pose questions? I don't even really want any answers. But there are questions.

M: Asking questions is such a simple thing, but it's not simplistic. What is the message?

S: There's a person I met at the art gallery at the time of the theft, when Irene's angel photograph was stolen. This person was broken. He'd experienced something so awful and prolonged and hideous in childhood. He said something like this: "This same thing that happened to me, probably has happened to hundreds of others. But I can only think about me. I don't know about them. I'm never not thinking about me. And there is nothing that will ever change this thing, and so I will always be this way. I hate everyone and I hate myself and I fold myself up inside very small, and then I try to poison myself with alcohol because it's the only way out that I can see."

M: A slow and painful death.

S: He was already dead, in his mind.

A: But he had come to this art exhibition of angels. He'd found himself there.

S: There were people that came to the exhibition who were barely holding it together. I didn't expect that. I wanted to make some kind of esoteric and distanced piece. I wanted to be at arm's length, as an observer, a recorder. But it was very emotional. I found it to be difficult. It was the most harrowing piece of art that I've constructed. I don't think I even knew that at the time. I was trying to be impartial, to just witness. But that's a ridiculous phrase, isn't it, "just witness."

216

M: Yes, it's never merely witnessing. It changes your DNA. It changes your eyes at some molecular level (whether that's scientifically possible or not, I don't know).

A: This is always when I feel as though art is useless. I mean, it's not, but also, it is. I believe in the power of art to transform lives. But I know also that a bowl of soup can be more useful.

S: The reason I mentioned this man who was broken is because he was there. What drew him? Why was this exhibit of angels important to him? When he was there, he seemed to grow increasingly angry, unhappy. And then he cried. He was agitated. And then he also retreated into himself. Did it help? Did it hurt? I don't know. I never saw him again.

A: This is how it is with people, with encounters. They move away from us, and we don't know what happens next. We're only ever seeing part of a story.

M: I suppose that's what I want to get at in my film. This sense that there are no endings. We can hold things together for a while and make them seem to cohere, as we write novels, tell stories in film. But in reality, they leak out in all directions. There is an ongoingness that I wish to convey. The traditional narrative arc is wonderful, and useful, but it is not the only mode in which to talk about how things occur, how life rolls out, how life comes at us and is so boring and delightful at once, so unpredictable and so obvious, so weird and so lovely and hidden and open. Our stories are so delicate and at times invisible or vulnerable. Sometimes pictures tell them better, or whispers, or fragments, or unconnected descriptions of things and songs and moments.

S: I'm interested, too, if I may say, in how we put ourselves into these stories we're telling. Trying to tell. So, when I was accumulating my observations and anecdotes and responses in my Angel Project at the art gallery, I realized in the end that it was really all about me, though I really had conscientiously focused outwardly.

M: Yes. Whatever we make is going to be interpreted through who we are, what we've seen to that point, what we've been through, what we find to be missing in ourselves, what holes we are trying to fill, what we desire, hope for, and dream about.

A: And then isn't it interesting the way that we are just sometimes inexplicably drawn to a subject? Irene Guernsey, for example. That we've all ended up in this same room, talking, is a bit of a miracle, a bit of a gift, isn't it? I'm quite astounded, quite astonished, to be sitting here with the two of you, in all honesty. I sometimes find myself leaning back in my chair and giving my head a bit of a shake. You're in my home!

M: And it's wonderful.

S: When we're talking, I don't think, oh my God, I'm in the room with a movie star—*the* Michelangelo Dupree. But after, there's a pause and we turn off our recording device, and you know, when we're just sitting there quiet for a while, looking at each other. I forget for the first bit, but then it hits me, and I have to stop myself from saying something really stupid. I'm sorry, but it's true. I kind of freak out a bit inside.

M: That will completely go away though, the more you get to know me.

S: And then you say something like that, and I think, what, why me?

A: I'm the same, I completely confess. You're royalty and I'm a commoner.

[Laughter.]

M: I'm not! I'm not! Truly!

A: You're a bit more like the angels who descend unannounced. You're not ordinary.

M: And what I'm more interested in than almost anything is what it is to be ordinary.

A: But angels aren't ordinary.

M: They seek out ordinary people. Maybe they are ordinary people.

A: They also seem to bestow things on certain people who are anything but ordinary. Okay. Let's think, though. Do rich people need angels? Do celebrities? Do they believe in them? Or people who are blessed with extraordinary good looks? Do you know what I mean? Or talents. Talents. What do they need from angels?

S: What do any of us need?

M: Do we create angels to fill a need? Are they there because we need them?

A: We invent what we need.

M: Which doesn't mean they don't exist. Just not in the usual ways we imagine.

A: You seem like an angel to me.

S: Yes.

M: Me? But you seem like angels to me.

A: I look at you and you have this aura around you. I swear. Is that what they call star power?

S: You have star power, definitely. That expression, "wattage," applies. You have a presence, charisma. You're larger than life, as they say, also. It's real!

M: That's lovely of you to say, really, but when I look at the two of you, I feel there's something radiating, as well. I mean it. We've talked about what it is to be so-called "ordinary," but you're anything but.

A: We're having a love-in!

[Laughter.]

M: When women get together this happens, though, when we really listen to each other and look at each other. It's simply that. That's what's happening. And I really do believe, if I can be said to be a believer, I believe that everything affects everyone. What we're doing here has meaning. This is where meaning is found, where it arises.

A: What would we give up to enact this again? How can others find this space? Is making our own space enough?

I suppose, for the record, we should say that while we've been talking, we've been growing wings. We've turned the

recording device off now and again. We've taken breaks. There have been growing pains. And our wings are quite different, one from the other, but they're also similar.

M: We're not Victoria's Secret angels walking down the runway.

S: No, we are not.

[Laughter.]

A: Do either of you want to say anything else for the recorder? You're both shaking your heads. We've talked enough. Yes, then, shall we? Go outside? Try these things out? Let's stretch our wings. Let's fly.

M: Yes.

S: Yes.

Questionnaire for the Reader

Describe your wings.

_____

_____

_____

_____

_____

_____

_____

_____

_____

_____

_____

_____

_____

_____

_____

_____

_____

_____

_____

What miracles have you performed?

_____

_____

_____

_____

_____

_____

_____

_____

_____

_____

_____

_____

_____

Describe someone who changed your life.

_____

_____

_____

_____

_____

_____

_____

_____

_____

_____

_____

_____

_____

Who have you hurt? How?

_____

_____

_____

_____

_____

_____

_____

_____

_____

_____

_____

_____

_____

Who has hurt you? How?

_____

_____

_____

_____

_____

_____

_____

_____

_____

_____

_____

_____

_____

Describe an event in your life that changed you. How are you different because of it?

_____

_____

_____

_____

_____

_____

_____

_____

_____

_____

_____

_____

_____

Do you agree that "everything affects everyone"?

_____

_____

_____

_____

_____

_____

_____

_____

_____

_____

_____

_____

_____

Where do you want to be in five years?

_____
_____
_____
_____
_____
_____
_____
_____
_____
_____
_____
_____
_____
_____

Contemplate the following statements and write anything you want after reading them:

It ain't no sin to dream and to feel joy.

_____
_____
_____
_____
_____
_____
_____
_____
_____
_____
_____
_____
_____

If I could lay my fears aside for one day, I'd have the nerve to be happy.

_____
_____
_____
_____
_____
_____
_____
_____
_____
_____
_____
_____
_____

There are new ways to live that are possible to invent and that will brighten your soul.

_____
_____
_____
_____
_____
_____
_____
_____
_____
_____
_____
_____
_____

Words are also winged creatures.

_____
_____
_____
_____
_____
_____
_____
_____
_____
_____
_____
_____
_____
_____

The secret of life is me or it is a little bird or a feather.

_____
_____
_____
_____
_____
_____
_____
_____
_____
_____
_____
_____
_____
_____
_____

And the message is...

_____

_____

_____

_____

_____

_____

_____

_____

_____

_____

_____

_____

_____

Each of us is responsible for the entire world.

_____

_____

_____

_____

_____

_____

_____

_____

_____

_____

_____

_____

_____

Shawna
Cry a Hallelujah for Me, *or* A Soliloquy of the Irrational Dark

Do not read what I write as a reader would do.
Unless this reader works, he too, on the soliloquies
of the irrational dark.

—Clarice Lispector

When you have finished this book cry a hallelujah
for me.

—Clarice Lispector

One last soliloquy, then.

I travelled to Rome because that is where the angels are. I had been to Rome twice before, once in 1995 on my honeymoon and once in November of 2018; this last time was in November of 2019. Since then, I like to write and think

about their presence and to try to sit in a chair, alone, in a room, and to feel them, to see if they travelled back with me, to my home in the suburbs of Edmonton.

Of course they have. I have come to believe that looking at light, experiencing it—this too is an angel. That one's own simple existence, pared down and quiet and true—that too is an angel.

All my life, at least once a year, someone has called me an angel. It has happened in bookstores and at the library where I currently work. It has happened to me several times, more than several, during the writing of this book, and each time it has shocked me. I walked out of myself then. Did they know I was writing a book about angels? Were they an angel? Each time someone asked me if I was an angel, I knew I was in the presence of an angel. It was a bit of a shock, the way we would look into each other's eyeballs, oh!

In my childhood I was surrounded by angels all the time. And for an interval they were everywhere for me. They didn't disappear, and I didn't stop believing in them. But I've been guilty of keeping them all to myself. This is because I didn't necessarily know to call them angels. Every minute of my life I have been surrounded by a swarm of angels like bees, or blue flowers like butterflies, that sing heaven in an "Ahhhhh, ahhhhh, ahhhhh."

I can't always see them or feel them anymore, but to not feel them is also feeling them. Writing them is feeling them. One can feel angels into being.

The wings of an angel can be two pieces of crumpled paper.

The wings of an angel can be branches of a tree, green-feathered, or gold and red.

The wings of an angel can be open books, or wings painted on a wall, whatever you see when you close your eyes and imagine.

Remember being a child and imagining what it would be like to fly? You were an angel then.

When I was eight, I would walk home from school for lunch, and I would be so slow that I would have to eat quickly and turn around and go back. The reason for this was that I imagined I was flying home, and in my mind's eye I was a winged creature, flying above myself, careening through the sky, shooting up and around and in lovely dancing circles. How I loved flying! And how I loved my wings! So this slowed my earthly pace.

In Rome we visited the Ponte Sant'Angelo, the "Bridge of Angels," many times. We visited the Biblioteca Angelica, which has nothing to do with angels, they say, but is named for Bishop Angelo Rocca, a writer and book collector in the sixteenth century. We visited the church designed by Michelangelo—Santa Maria degli Angeli e dei Martiri. We followed a trace of angel wings each day. We saw hundreds and hundreds of angels. There were as many angel wings as there are butterfly wings in the gathering of monarchs in migration. Maybe more. I photographed angel wings in churches, and I surreptitiously felt the feathers of angel statues used to support holy-water fonts. I breathed in the colours of all the variations of angel wings in fresco, oil paint, mosaic. The way the angel wings caught the light: I noticed this again and again. I relinquished in myself any of the hierarchies of angels and embraced them all equally, and they embraced me. I fell backwards into the wings of angels. This is what one does when one has reached the illuminated core in the darkness of one's own being, the old glory of existing, the thump of the heart, the holy *I am*, the love of one's own heart, the *I am is*, the nothing, the everything, the early-morning flower of one's own being, the eternal *thank you*.

Have you experienced a state of grace? Maybe, as Clarice Lispector has said, experiencing a state of grace is like awaiting an annunciation.

Let us say that there is a state of grace that is like awaiting an annunciation. And the message? The gift?

Whose soul are you responsible for? What will you do to harbour the intimate secrets and dreams of that person? How can you cultivate the serenity necessary to receive the message? I'm not talking about God here, unless you understand God as being you.

Don't be afraid of being an angel. Don't be afraid of the angel in you, that winged ghost. Don't be afraid of saying things that don't fit into the conversation. Start a new conversation. Keep adding to the large conversation that is life and living. It won't be continuous, but will happen in episodes, and like a film or a long poem, you can cut the scenes and stanzas that you know instinctively don't belong. It's your film, and later, when the editors and executives or whomever has power over your creative work want you to cut other things, you must resist, because in twenty years someone will get it. You'll get it. Maybe thirty years, maybe a hundred. No one really matters except the person who pulls it out of an attic or a buckled cardboard box.

What I wanted to learn in writing this book—and this *is* part of the book—what I am writing to you this instant: angels are life. If you're looking for an all-encompassing definition, I repeat: an angel is your life. Your life is an angel. You are responsible for all the other angels, responsible to life. Your life is a message; the angel announces this every second of every day. And it says: *hallelujah*.

The Whole Time I've Been Writing This

They come on to my clean
sheet of paper and leave a Rorschach blot.

—Anne Sexton, from "The Fallen Angels"

I've also been scribbling pictures of angels.

Inspired perhaps by Paul Klee's *Angelus Novus*. Inspired by Fra Angelico's annunciations. By a particular Rembrandt drawing. When we were in Rome, I took countless photographs of angels and their wings. Of Klee's angel, Walter Benjamin famously said that the angel is

> looking as though he is about to move away from something he is fixedly contemplating. His eyes are staring, his mouth is open, his wings are spread. This is how one pictures the angel of history. His face is turned toward the past. Where we perceive a chain of events, he sees one single catastrophe which keeps piling wreckage

upon wreckage and hurls it in front of his feet. The angel would like to stay, awaken the dead, and make whole what has been smashed. But a storm is blowing from Paradise; it has got caught in his wings with such violence that the angel can no longer close them. This storm irresistibly propels him into the future to which his back is turned, while the pile of debris before him grows skyward. This storm is what we call progress.

There are so many kinds of angels; we've invented one for just about everything. And in each angel's wings, the storms from paradise are caught.

I'm not an artist, but I put my black felt pen to the white page and I let it move, I let it move me. I tell the pen to make me an angel like Fra Angelico's. I don't lift the pen until I'm done with the small drawing. None of them look like anything—certainly not a Fra Angelico—but while I'm drawing, I'm picturing in my mind the colours of the individual feathers, the flow and drapery of the angel's garments. An angel is here to tell us things and we only need to listen. In the scribbled tangle of the wings, I imagine storms, yes, but connections, small breezes, soft rain, gentle snow. One scribble leads to another one, one wing reaching out to another and failing to touch. Wings flutter though, and even the merest flapping sends out alterations in the air, carrying the secret message, the message that every life sends out even without knowing it.

The wing of an angel is a reminder that the sky is wide open. Substances alter. If you can fly, you must fly. If you have bird power, you must embrace the sky.

If, as Bachelard says, you can succumb to a reverie of flight, then there is a "great opening, a wide opening." The world, he says, must fly. Flying is your destiny. Dominate the sky.

To fly you can also move the pen across a page, which is its own kind of flight. You scroll and scribble and scrape

and twirl and flit and fritter and loop-de-loop and pause and swoosh and loll and never once raise the tip of the pen from the page, and then, when you do, the nib is in the air and it connects to all the other airborne pens, hovering, haloing. At least there is that undeniable connection, the thought above the page, that cloud that halo that shadow.

Ah, but you writers, you readers, why would you stay seated when you can get up and fly?

The recipe for flight is within you. But you can find it in books, too, or in your dream from last night. The cerulean sky is one potion or elixir. The spine from the top of the Rocky Mountains. For black wings, fling yourself into the darkness; for white ones, the ocean foam. For wings of many colours, fly low over cities at the golden hour.

Let us end this by taking flight. This is such a useful act of very solid happiness and kindness. Why isn't this promoted by self-help gurus and those scholars of uplift?

You, rise, and I shall take your photograph.

Permissions

Annunciation 1443 FRA ANGELICO Wiki Visual Art Encyclopedia.

Annunciation 1442 FRA ANGELICO Wiki Visual Art Encyclopedia.

Inv. 4840 (*Left Wing of a Blue Roller*) DÜRER ALBRECHT reproduced with permission from The Albertina Museum, Vienna.

Works Cited

Alan Watts, *The Wisdom of Insecurity*, 2011, Vintage Books.

Walter Benjamin, "On the Concept of History," https://www.sfu.ca/~andrewf/CONCEPT2.html.

Acknowledgements

Thank you Aimée Parent Dunn, wonderful editor, publisher and human being. Thank you Ellie Hastings for the perfect cover design. Thank you Theo Hummer for such care with the copy edits.

Thank you to friends in art and writing for all the conversations that mean everything.

This book is dedicated to Rob Lemay and Chloe Lemay and to all my library angel friends at Woodcroft, one of whom is even, unsurprisingly, named Angela.

Thank you to the Alberta Foundation for the Arts and Canada Council for the Arts for your support.

Thank you to Charles Simic for permission to use his poem, "In the Library."

Shawna Lemay is the author of *The Flower Can Always Be Changing* (shortlisted for the 2019 Wilfred Eggleston Award for Non-Fiction) and the novel, *Rumi and the Red Handbag*, which made Harper's Bazaar's #THELIST. She has also written multiple books of poetry, a book of essays, and the experimental novel *Hive*. *All the God-Sized Fruit*, her first book, won the Stephan G. Stephansson Award and the Gerald Lampert Memorial Award. *Calm Things: Essays* was shortlisted for the Wilfred Eggleston Award for Non-Fiction. She lives in Edmonton.

Everything Affects Everyone